This book is for all those who were born around midwinter and were told they would be getting their Christmas and birthday presents in one this year! These stories are my special present to you all — C. M.
For Melissa Robinson, with much love — H. C.

Barefoot Books
2067 Massachusetts Ave
Cambridge, MA 02140

Barefoot Books
294 Banbury Road
Oxford, OX2 7ED

First published in Great Britain by Barefoot Books, Ltd
and in the United States of America by Barefoot Books, Inc in 2007
This hardback edition first published in 2015

Graphic design by Barefoot Books
Reproduction by Bright Arts, Singapore
Printed in China on 100% acid-free paper
This book was typeset in Bernhard Modern, Caslon Old Face
Caslon Open Face and Albertina MT
The illustrations were prepared in watercolour
and mixed media on Arches paper

ISBN 978-1-78285-251-3

British Cataloguing-in-Publication Data:
a catalogue record for this book is available from the British Library

Library of Congress Cataloging-in-Publication Data
is available under LCCN 2006100360

1 3 5 7 9 8 6 4 2

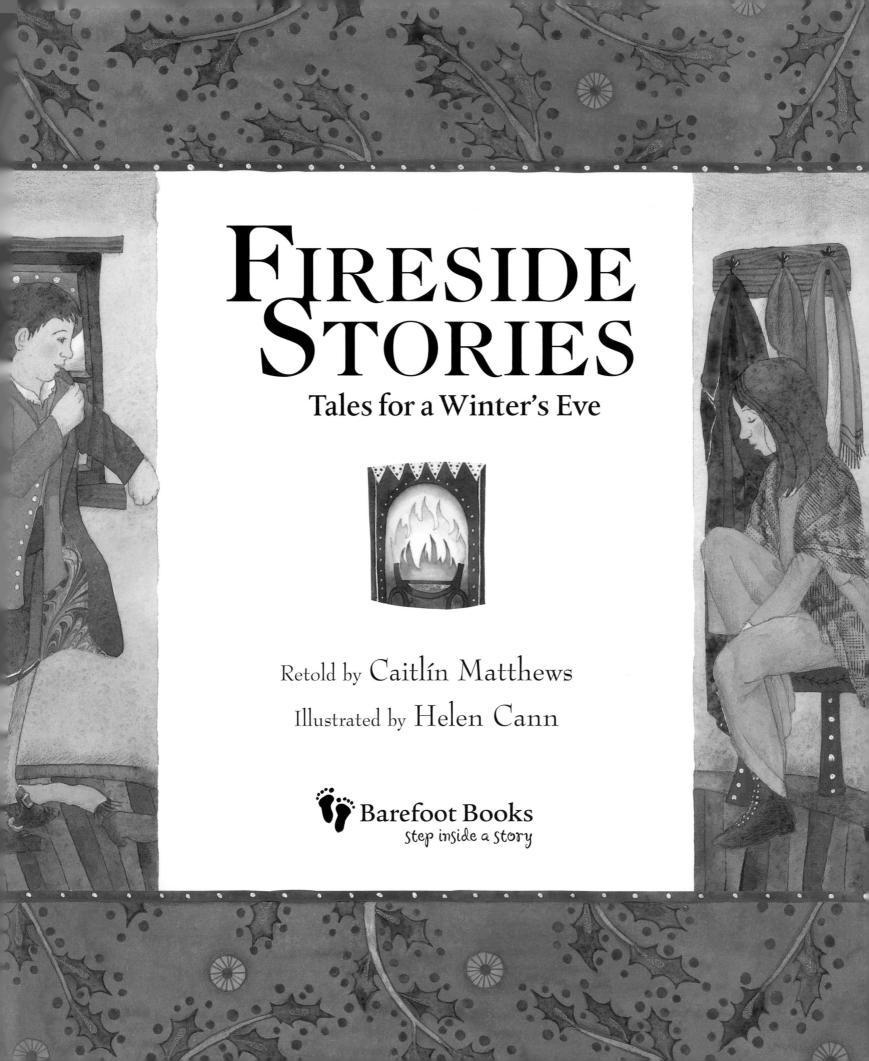

FIRESIDE STORIES

Tales for a Winter's Eve

Retold by Caitlín Matthews

Illustrated by Helen Cann

Barefoot Books

step inside a story

BY THE FIRESIDE

When the nights grow long and the days grow short, when summer is a distant memory and the cold and darkness of winter an ever-present reality, it is good to sit by the fireside and tell stories. The fire has a special magic. As we peer deeply into the red, glowing embers, we remember the stories from before our own time. We see castles and forests, the dens of witches and monsters, the path of the hero over rivers of flame, and smouldering caves where gold and jewels are hidden.

Stories make us feel safe, stories give us wisdom. And there is no better time for stories than in the winter. In some cultures, it is considered unlucky to tell stories about snow and winter at another time of year, or when there is no

snow upon the ground. Why is this? Is it because there is a special blessing upon the winter months when life can be so hard for plants, trees, animals and humans alike? Or is it because this special time of ice and snow is where we find our greatest strength and wisdom?

Midwinter is the time of gathering together because, as the sun grows fainter and lower in the sky, so the days grow shorter and the nights longer. Even in the distant days of our ancestors, it was a time of gifts and of meetings with friends and family long parted. From our ancestors, all those mothers and fathers and sisters and brothers, we have learned how to make the year turn once more. We gather together at the time of greatest darkness and greatest need to make a brave show of our hopes and longings. Instead of complaining about the cold, we bring in the evergreens of pine, holly and mistletoe to remind us of the far-off spring. Instead of fasting on a tiny handful of crumbs, we make a feast of the best food and drink we have in the house. Instead of sitting in the dark, we build up the fire and put up decorations that shine in the dancing light.

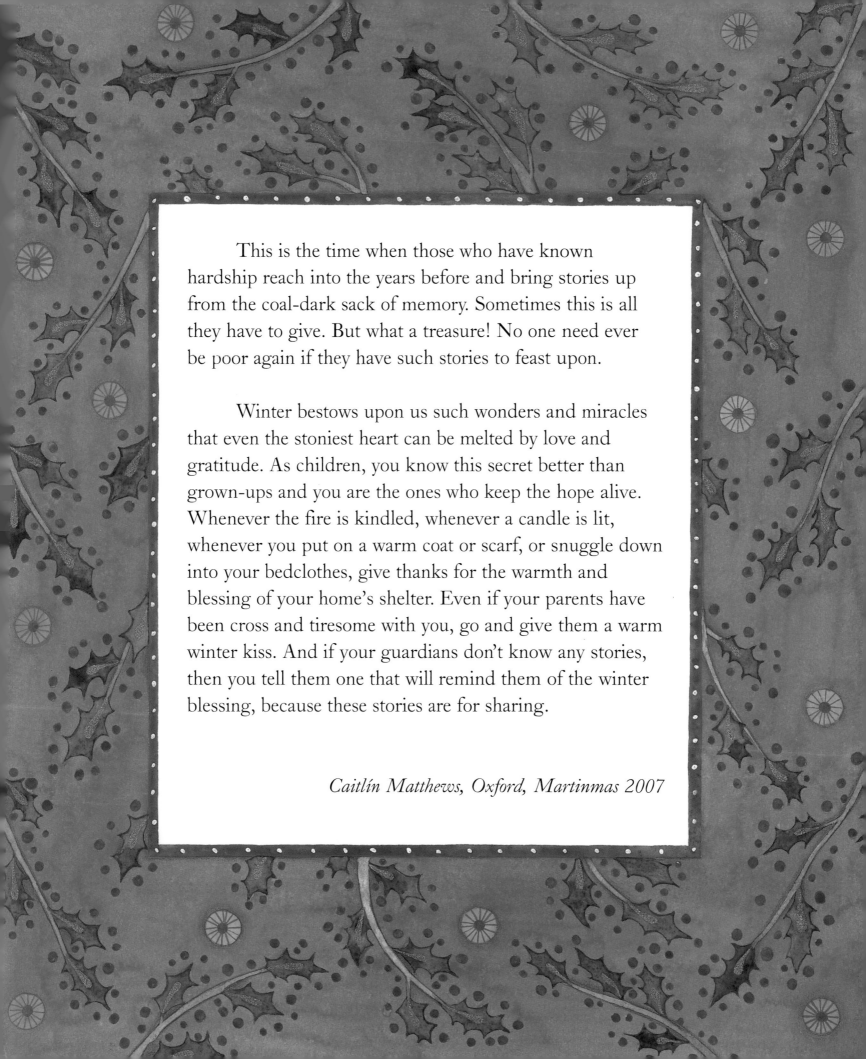

This is the time when those who have known hardship reach into the years before and bring stories up from the coal-dark sack of memory. Sometimes this is all they have to give. But what a treasure! No one need ever be poor again if they have such stories to feast upon.

Winter bestows upon us such wonders and miracles that even the stoniest heart can be melted by love and gratitude. As children, you know this secret better than grown-ups and you are the ones who keep the hope alive. Whenever the fire is kindled, whenever a candle is lit, whenever you put on a warm coat or scarf, or snuggle down into your bedclothes, give thanks for the warmth and blessing of your home's shelter. Even if your parents have been cross and tiresome with you, go and give them a warm winter kiss. And if your guardians don't know any stories, then you tell them one that will remind them of the winter blessing, because these stories are for sharing.

Caitlín Matthews, Oxford, Martinmas 2007

THE STORIES

The festival of Hallowe'en, or All Hallows' Eve, on 31 October, marks the time when the dark half of the year begins, heralding the return of winter. Among the Celtic and Gaelic peoples of Scotland and Ireland, this festival is known as Samhain (pronounced 'Sow'en') or Summer's End. Hallowe'en is followed by All Hallows' Day, or All Saints' Day, on 1 November.

At Hallowe'en, the doors between the world we know and the world we cannot see are said to be open. Traditionally, it is the time when the clutter of the past year is cleared out or burned. Nowadays, many people still celebrate Hallowe'en by making pumpkin lanterns and by putting candles and lights in their windows to help the ancestors to find their way home. It's a time for fancy dress costumes, for fortune-telling, and for traditional games such as apple-bobbing and trick-or-treating. And of course, Hallowe'en is a special night for stories of strange happenings, like this one.

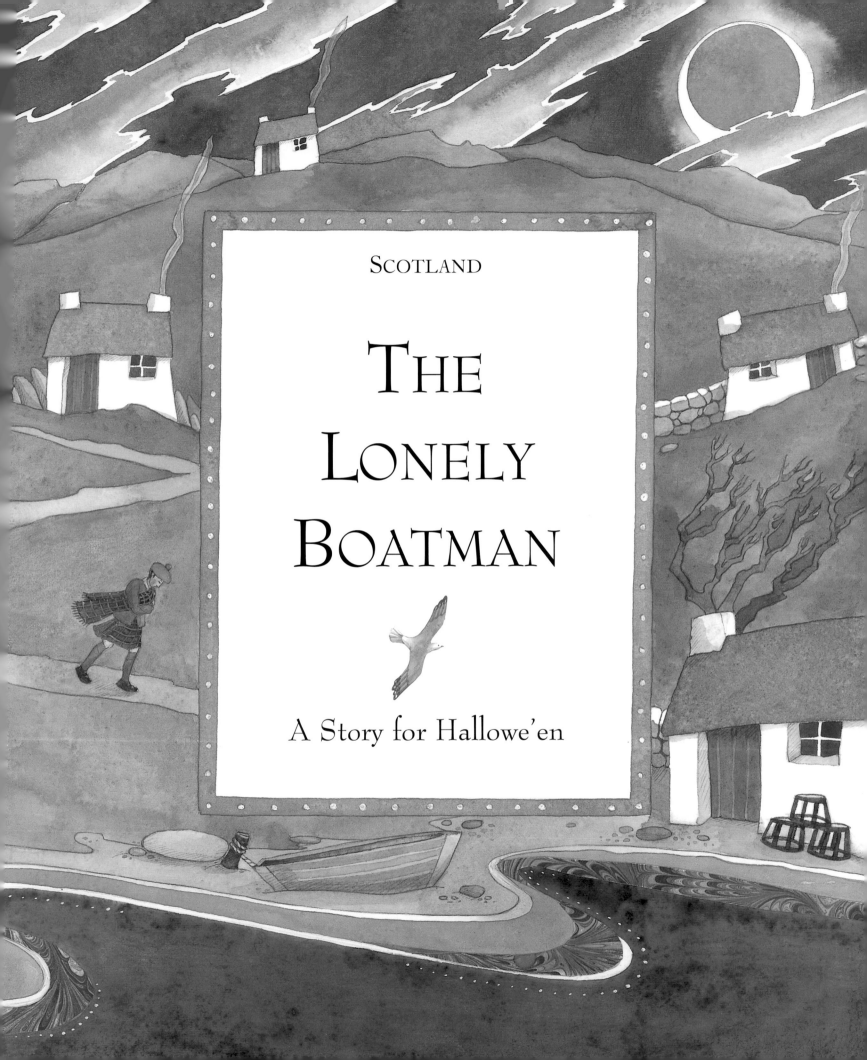

SCOTLAND

THE
LONELY
BOATMAN

A Story for Hallowe'en

A long time ago in Scotland, there lived a shy and lonely fisherman called Hamish. One Hallowe'en, when all the people of the village were invited to a feast at the house of his clan chief, Hamish made his way through the windy darkness. It was a scary night to be outside, for the spirits of the dead were believed to visit their families on this festival, but inside the great hall there was feasting and merriment. Hamish sat quietly in a corner and ate his fill, saying nothing as usual, but nodding greetings to his neighbours. It was good to be in the company of many people on such a night and not in his little stone house all alone.

The Chieftain rose and gave the toast: 'Good health and long life! Peace upon the dead and prosperity upon the living!' Everyone drank deeply of the golden, peaty water of life. 'Now,' said the Chieftain. 'Since it is the night of Samhain, let us have songs and stories that will see us through to the morning light, for no one will sleep this night! If you have eaten at my table, then I ask that you each share a story or song. No one is excused. And the person who tells the best story will receive a purse of gold.'

Hamish's heart sank. He was not a man of many words, and was too shy to speak up in gatherings like this. As the storytelling harp went round the hall and got nearer and nearer, he shrank

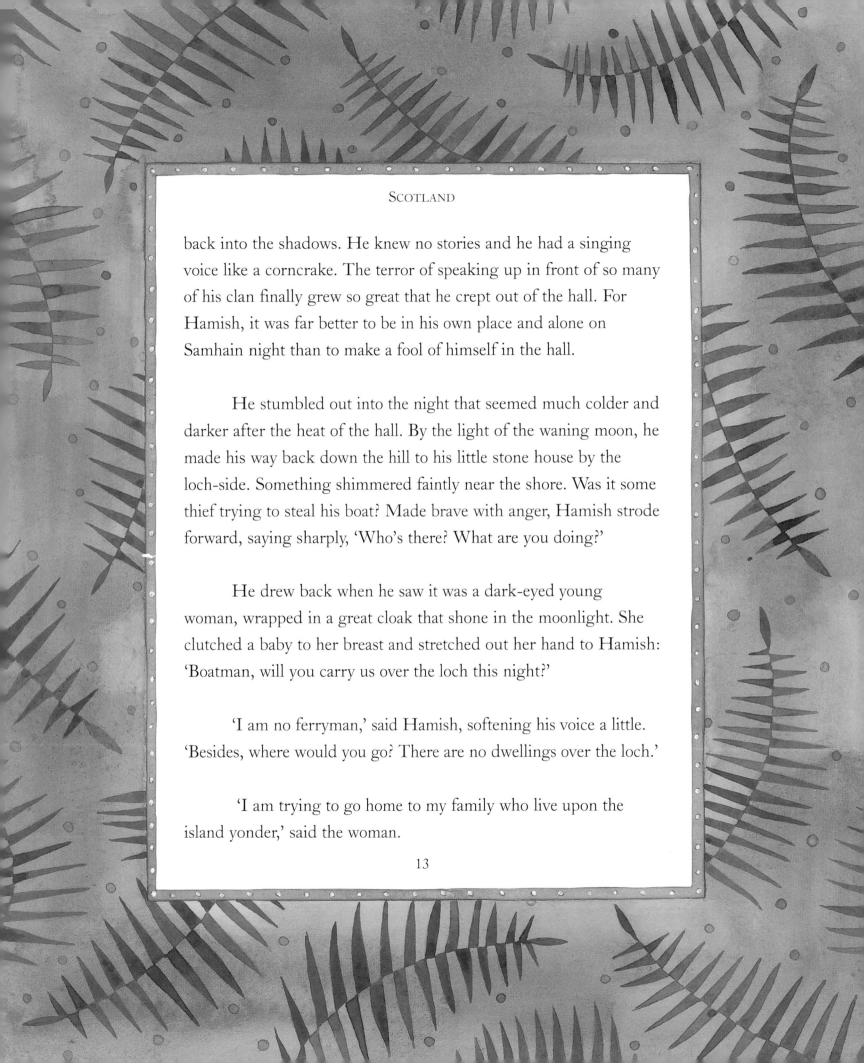

back into the shadows. He knew no stories and he had a singing voice like a corncrake. The terror of speaking up in front of so many of his clan finally grew so great that he crept out of the hall. For Hamish, it was far better to be in his own place and alone on Samhain night than to make a fool of himself in the hall.

He stumbled out into the night that seemed much colder and darker after the heat of the hall. By the light of the waning moon, he made his way back down the hill to his little stone house by the loch-side. Something shimmered faintly near the shore. Was it some thief trying to steal his boat? Made brave with anger, Hamish strode forward, saying sharply, 'Who's there? What are you doing?'

He drew back when he saw it was a dark-eyed young woman, wrapped in a great cloak that shone in the moonlight. She clutched a baby to her breast and stretched out her hand to Hamish: 'Boatman, will you carry us over the loch this night?'

'I am no ferryman,' said Hamish, softening his voice a little. 'Besides, where would you go? There are no dwellings over the loch.'

'I am trying to go home to my family who live upon the island yonder,' said the woman.

Hamish was puzzled, for this small island lay in the middle of the great loch, but there were no buildings there, only a huddle of grey stones that leaned together like women gossiping. He looked at her and decided that he should assist the poor woman, who had no other means of reaching the island. He helped her into his boat and rowed her over.

The oars sent ripples of pale moonlight in the dark lake waters, while the woman sat silently in the boat with her baby. Hamish shyly admired her, as he rowed, for she was very beautiful. As soon as they landed she ran quickly towards a little house that Hamish had never seen before. Three old women came out and welcomed the woman and her baby with cries of joy.

'Hamish, will you not come in and take a drink and eat with us for your service?' said the woman.

'Who are you to know my name when I have not given it?' he asked.

The woman threw back her cloak hood and the moonlight poured over her dark hair: 'I am Shula and this is my mother and her sisters. Come in and be welcome this night.'

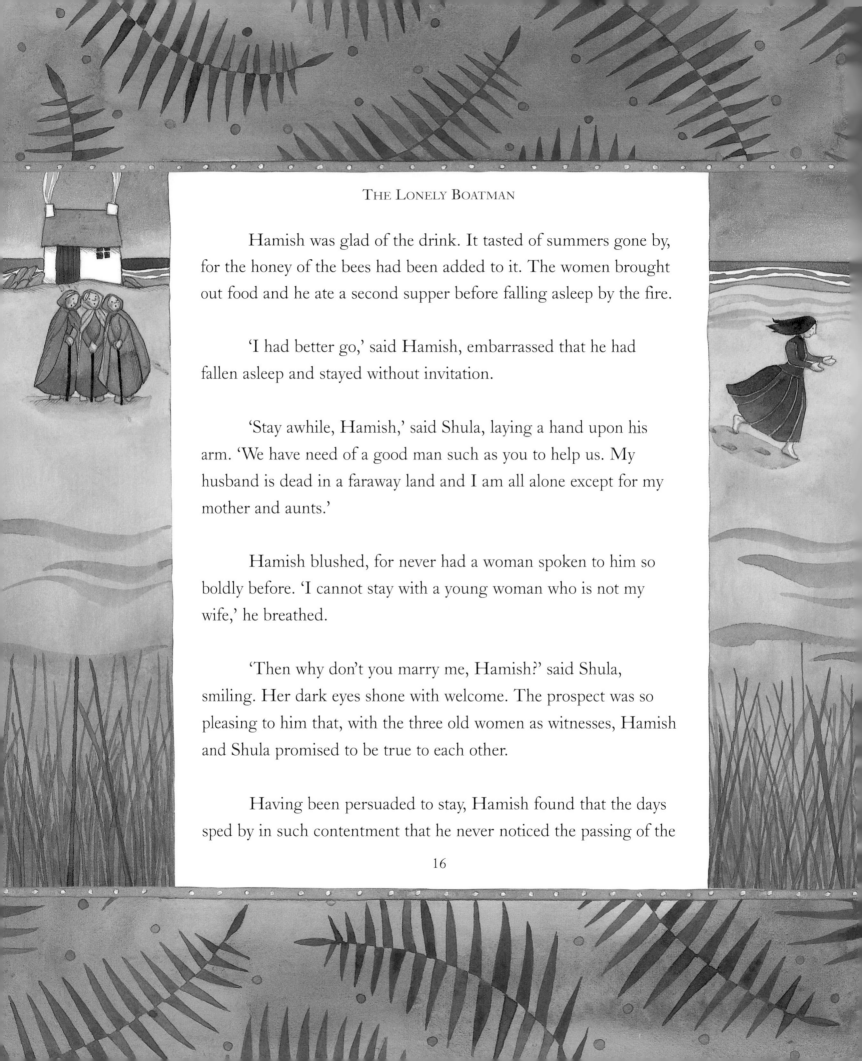

Hamish was glad of the drink. It tasted of summers gone by, for the honey of the bees had been added to it. The women brought out food and he ate a second supper before falling asleep by the fire.

'I had better go,' said Hamish, embarrassed that he had fallen asleep and stayed without invitation.

'Stay awhile, Hamish,' said Shula, laying a hand upon his arm. 'We have need of a good man such as you to help us. My husband is dead in a faraway land and I am all alone except for my mother and aunts.'

Hamish blushed, for never had a woman spoken to him so boldly before. 'I cannot stay with a young woman who is not my wife,' he breathed.

'Then why don't you marry me, Hamish?' said Shula, smiling. Her dark eyes shone with welcome. The prospect was so pleasing to him that, with the three old women as witnesses, Hamish and Shula promised to be true to each other.

Having been persuaded to stay, Hamish found that the days sped by in such contentment that he never noticed the passing of the

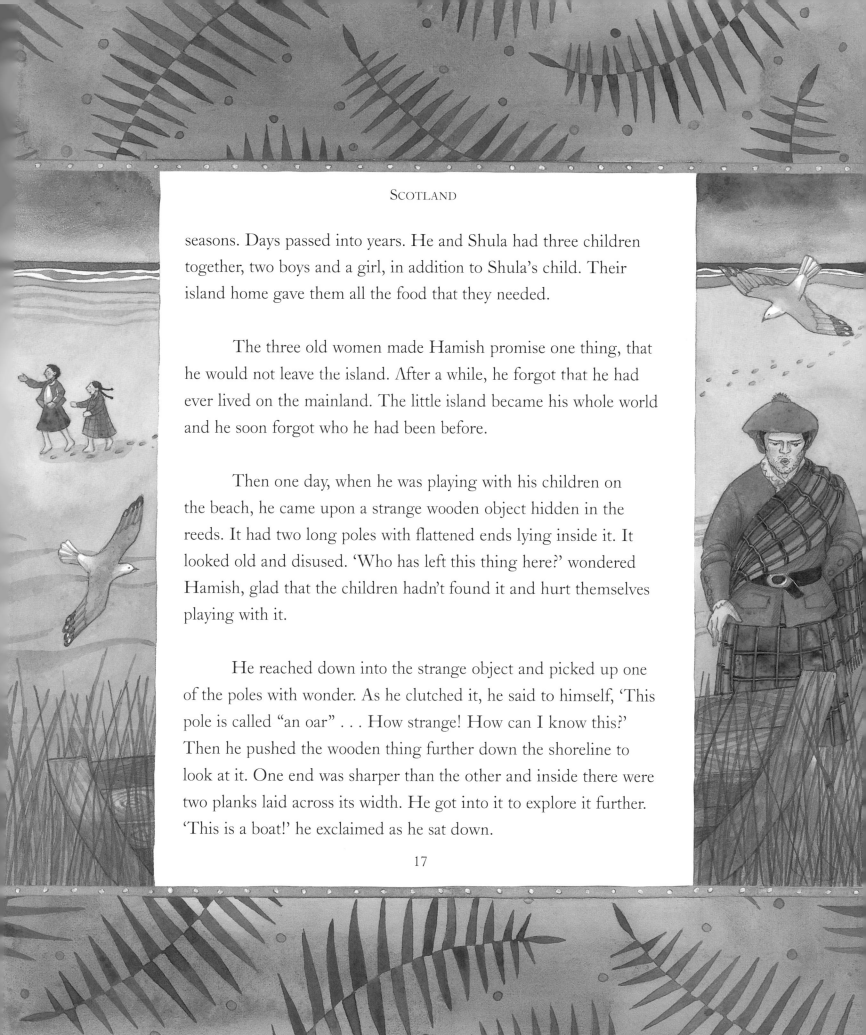

seasons. Days passed into years. He and Shula had three children together, two boys and a girl, in addition to Shula's child. Their island home gave them all the food that they needed.

The three old women made Hamish promise one thing, that he would not leave the island. After a while, he forgot that he had ever lived on the mainland. The little island became his whole world and he soon forgot who he had been before.

Then one day, when he was playing with his children on the beach, he came upon a strange wooden object hidden in the reeds. It had two long poles with flattened ends lying inside it. It looked old and disused. 'Who has left this thing here?' wondered Hamish, glad that the children hadn't found it and hurt themselves playing with it.

He reached down into the strange object and picked up one of the poles with wonder. As he clutched it, he said to himself, 'This pole is called "an oar" . . . How strange! How can I know this?' Then he pushed the wooden thing further down the shoreline to look at it. One end was sharper than the other and inside there were two planks laid across its width. He got into it to explore it further. 'This is a boat!' he exclaimed as he sat down.

17

His children came running excitedly along the shore as they watched their father push the boat into the loch. Coiled up in the prow of the boat was a net. 'I am a fisherman!' cried Hamish, beginning to remember. With great pleasure, he felt the pull of the oars under his hands and the way the boat answered and shot forward into the deep waters of the loch. He rowed and rowed, turning occasionally to wave to his children, who waved back at him.

Suddenly his boat struck against the shore of the mainland. Hamish jumped out of the boat ready to push it back into the water and return. But as soon as his foot touched the shore, day became night. He struggled to adjust his sight. Peering into the dimness of the waning moon, he found a little stone house by the shore that he remembered. Memory flooded back, as he recognised his own house from another life. Confused and anxious, he peered back over the dark lake. All he could see of the island under moonlight were grey stones huddled together — no house, no wife, no children.

Hamish burst into tears, torn and confused by memories of different times and events. Now he remembered this night. This was the same Samhain night when he had set off towards the island with his mysterious passenger and her baby many years ago. He had forgotten all about his earlier life.

Unable to bear the loss of his family, Hamish leaped up the hill to the Chieftain's hall where the people were still telling stories and singing songs. He crashed into the hall, weeping and crying out, 'My family is lost! My wife and children are gone!'

Amid the hushed whispering in the hall — for everyone knew that Hamish lived alone and that he had no wife or children — the Chieftain kindly sat him down and gave him some more of the water of life: 'Hamish, calm down and tell us what you mean, man! We cannot understand you.'

Hamish poured out his story, about the woman and the passage over to the island, their marriage and the birth of their children. People listened with their mouths open, while Hamish kept stopping to wipe his eyes and lament.

'Then I rowed back to you here and it was the same night as when I had left, but I had been gone for years and years,' Hamish concluded, gulping through his sobs.

When he had finished his story, the intense silence was broken when everyone clapped and cheered as poor Hamish sobbed, bewildered, into his handkerchief.

The Chieftain slapped him on the back: 'Many stories have we heard this night, but Hamish's story was the best of all, do you not agree?' The people all nodded heartily. 'I award to him the purse of gold,' he said, giving a fat pouch to Hamish.

'But it's not a story, it's the truth!' cried Hamish in vain, letting the coins fall to the ground.

'Ach! indeed, Hamish, my good man. You made it sound so like the truth, we almost believed you!' said the Chieftain, picking up the spilled gold and giving it to Hamish once more.

Time and again, Hamish returned to the island to find his lost family but, though he searched every hollow and cleft, not the trace of a living soul could he find there.

Throughout his long life, Hamish never took another wife. He remained a lonely boatman who said little. But if you questioned him, he could only repeat the story that I have told to you.

It is said that if you go to that loch on Hallowe'en, you may still find Hamish waiting for his long-lost ghostly family, for they say it only happens once a year on Samhain night.

21

Today, many people who live in the developed world do not experience the cycle of the seasons in the same way that their grandparents did. However, for people in rural communities, it was and still is common practice to slaughter domestic animals at the end of the autumn, partly because it is expensive to feed and shelter livestock during the cold winter months, and partly because their meat is needed as food.

In this old Russian story, the animals are not going to let their owners' plans win the day! Instead of letting themselves be put in the pot, they escape to the woods, where they have to use their wits and join forces with each other to survive the harsh northern winter in the wild. Many stories and folk-customs about animals take place during the winter months, reminding us to be grateful for these creatures that we depend upon, while also recalling that many wild animals will only reveal their special powers in the depths of winter.

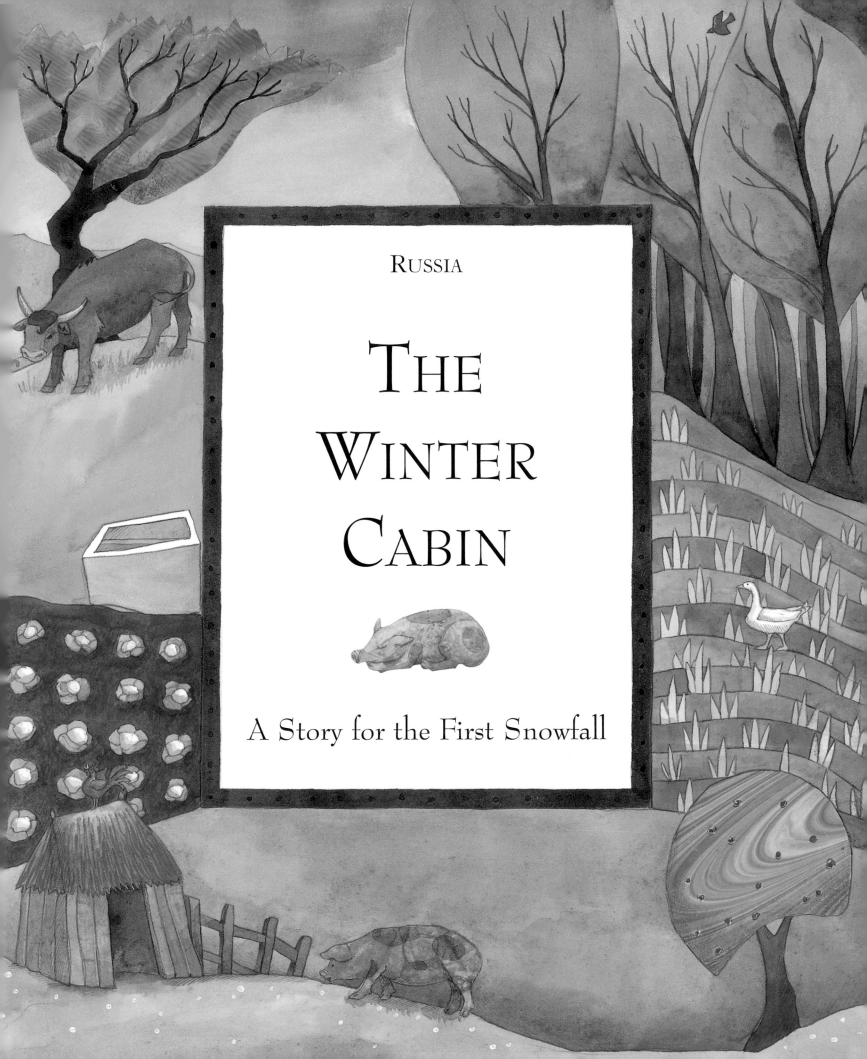

RUSSIA

THE
WINTER
CABIN

A Story for the First Snowfall

There was once an old peasant called Josef who kept a pig, a cockerel, a ram, a goose and an ox. There were guests coming for dinner that Sunday so Josef called to his wife, 'We will need some meat. I'll kill the cockerel tomorrow.'

The cockerel heard these words and quietly hid in the forest. When Josef went to find the bird, the cockerel had vanished. 'I can't find the cockerel! I shall have to kill the pig instead!' said Josef to his wife.

The pig looked up from her trough and ran squealing into the forest. The next day, Josef looked everywhere for her in vain. 'No cockerel, no pig — how very strange! Well, I shall just have to kill the ram instead.'

When the ram overheard this, he hurried to the goose. 'Quick!' he said. 'I'm off to the forest and, if you're wise, you'll come too.' And off to the forest they went.

The next day, Josef scoured the yard for the ram and the goose, but he couldn't find them anywhere. 'Well, wife, it looks as though we shall have to slaughter the ox, since none of the other beasts can be found.'

But the ox was not at all happy about becoming his master's
Sunday dinner, so he too set off as fast as his legs could carry him.
He found the other animals, and they all lived happily in the forest
that summer, eating whatever they liked, free to roam without a care
in the world. But summer soon turned to autumn and autumn
brought the cold winds and the first ice of the year.

'Listen, friends,' said the ox. 'Winter is coming and we must
seek shelter if we are to survive. The old man isn't going to come
out here and thatch the branches of the trees to keep us dry and
warm, you know. If we want to see another spring, we must build a
winter cabin for ourselves.'

The ram said, 'My thick woolly coat will keep me warm.'
The pig said, 'I shall dig a big hole and lie in the earth.'
'My soft feathers will be like a quilt,' said the goose.
'I can manage by roosting in a tree,' said the cockerel.

When the ox saw that none of the animals could be bothered
to help him, he set to and made a winter cabin out of wood. Inside,
he put a stove of stone and made his bed on top of it. Only a few
days later, autumn turned to winter. The winds sent down the first
snows and the animals in the forest began to look for shelter.

The ram's fleecy coat was soon covered in icicles and he banged with his horns on the door of the winter cabin. 'Brrrr, brrrr! Let me in!' he called.

From within the cosy cabin, the ox said, 'You didn't want to help me when I asked. You said your thick woolly coat would keep you warm.'

'Let me in, let me in! If you don't open up, I shall break down the door with my horns.'

'Goodness! I shall be cold without a door,' thought the ox. 'All right,' he said, 'in you come,' and he let the ram inside to warm himself on the bench beside the stove.

Soon the pig was at the door, her pink skin all pimply with cold. 'Oink-woink! Won't you let me in to warm myself?'

'I will not!' replied the ox. 'You said that you would keep warm by burrowing in the earth; you didn't want to help me.'

'If you don't let me in, I shall dig under the walls and the hut will fall down,' said the pig.

26

'Dear me!' thought the ox. 'Then we will be cold indeed. All right, in you come,' he said and he opened the door to let the pig inside. Down she went into the cellar where she curled up contentedly.

Next came the goose, her white feathers looking even paler with a covering of snowflakes upon them. 'Garak, garak! Let me come in!' she honked.

'But you said that your soft feathers would feel as warm as a quilt in the winter cold!' said the ox.

'If you don't let me in, I shall peck all the moss from the cracks in the windows and the wind will get into every corner.'

'Now that won't do,' thought the ox. 'There are enough draughts in this house already with me opening the door so much. All right, in you come,' he said and he let in the goose, who came and roosted on the post by the door.

Lastly, the cockerel came, with his feathers all blown about and sticking up like twigs. 'Corrock-cor-oo! I'm dying of cold out here! Let me come in!'

28

'I thought you were going to spend the winter in a tree,' said the ox. 'Besides, you didn't do anything to help me.'

'If you don't let me in soon, I shall scratch holes in the roof,' said the cockerel.

'We don't want the snow coming in,' thought the ox. 'All right, in you come,' he said and he let in the cockerel, who settled on a beam over the door.

And there the animals stayed in their winter cabin. The winter grew colder and the snow deeper. Soon other visitors were planning to visit the winter cabin, hungry visitors who wanted to eat the five friends. In the heart of the forest, a pack of wolves drew lots to see who would go into the winter cabin first. A wily old grey wolf won.

With his clever paws, the wolf was quick to open the cabin door. But his visit to the dark cabin was not at all what he expected! As soon as he was inside, the ox pinned him bodily to the wall with his long horns. The ram butted him in the side and the pig squealed up from the cellar in a bloodthirsty way, 'Skroink-woink! I'm sharpening the axe and the knife, ready to skin you alive!'

29

The goose rushed in and nipped the wolf very painfully on his behind, while the cockerel danced overhead screeching out, 'Give him to me. I'll hang him from the beam!'

The other wolves, who had been listening at the door, took to their heels in terror. The wily old grey wolf twisted and turned and yelped and scratched as he struggled to free himself. Leaving a great patch of fur between the ox's horns, he leaped away from the winter cabin with his tail between his legs. Never had he been so beaten up.

When he had rejoined his pack, the wolf related his adventures. 'I tell you friends, there are five monsters in that cabin! There was a huge peasant in a black shirt who knocked the breath out of me and hit me with clubs. Then there was a small, grey-coated fiend who punched me all over. A furious demon in a white cloak knocked nails into my behind, while a fearsome villain in a scarlet cap kept threatening to hang me up. As for the one who was sharpening the knives and axes to skin me, I shudder to think what he must have looked like!'

From that day on, the pack of wolves left the winter cabin and its monstrous occupants very much alone. The ox, the cockerel, the ram, the goose and the pig lived peacefully together that winter.

31

Before the arrival of Christianity in Europe, the shortest day and the longest night of the year, the Midwinter Solstice, was the major midwinter festival, celebrated on 21 December. However, for many centuries now, the festival has moved on a few days to mark the birth of Christ, starting on Christmas Eve (24 December) and continuing through until Christmas Day.

Christmas is a special time for families to come together to celebrate the season, often giving and receiving gifts and hanging up Christmas stockings, which will traditionally contain an orange for the sun, a silver sixpence for the moon and a piece of coal to light the fire and keep warm. In this magical Christmas Eve story from Austria, the three boys are too poor to hope for anything more than a decent meal to mark the arrival of their holiday. But then, while their father is out looking for work, there is a knock on the door and a very unusual guest enters their lives . . .

AUSTRIA

SCHNITZLE, SCHNOTZLE & SCHNOOTZLE

A Story for Christmas Eve

Many Christmases ago, there lived a poor cobbler and his three sons, Fritzel, Franzel and Hansel. His wife had died some years before and he struggled to feed his family. In good times, when the cobbler mended a farmer's Sunday shoes, they would drink good goat's milk. If he mended the baker's wife's shoes, they would eat a stick of crusty bread. If the butcher's shoes were to be mended, then they would have a rich stew in a big pot, with vegetables, noodles and herbs to make it tasty and filling.

And when they sat down for their stew, the cobbler would laugh and clap his hands together and proclaim, 'Well, boys! Today we have a good . . . Schnitzle, Schnotzle and Schnootzle.' And the boys would laugh with glee as their father ladled out the stew into each brimming bowl. They didn't care what their father called it, so long as there was more of the lovely stew to eat.

Those were the rich times, when they had full bellies. But a year came that was worse than all other years. War raged in their land. People had no money to spend so they went with unmended shoes, and the cobbler had little to give his children. In the summer and autumn, they could live off the land, for there were grains, berries and roots. But as December arrived, the land was stripped bare and the winter brought nothing but hunger.

34

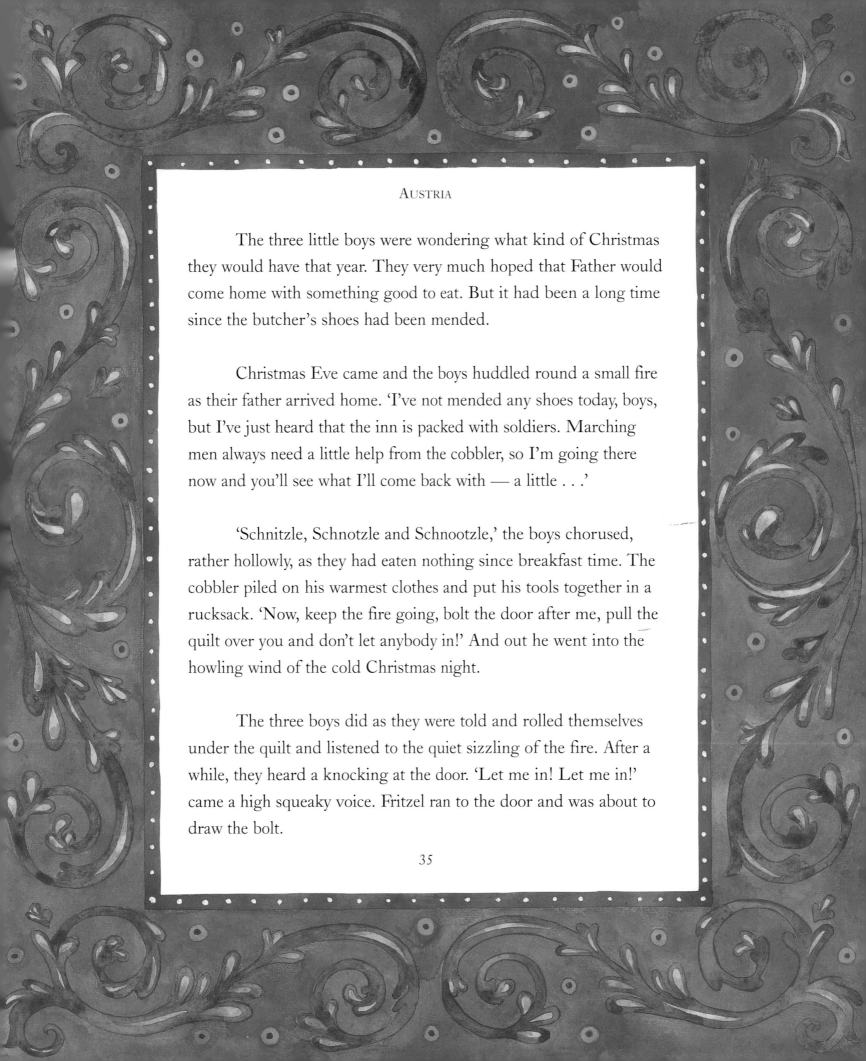

The three little boys were wondering what kind of Christmas they would have that year. They very much hoped that Father would come home with something good to eat. But it had been a long time since the butcher's shoes had been mended.

Christmas Eve came and the boys huddled round a small fire as their father arrived home. 'I've not mended any shoes today, boys, but I've just heard that the inn is packed with soldiers. Marching men always need a little help from the cobbler, so I'm going there now and you'll see what I'll come back with — a little . . .'

'Schnitzle, Schnotzle and Schnootzle,' the boys chorused, rather hollowly, as they had eaten nothing since breakfast time. The cobbler piled on his warmest clothes and put his tools together in a rucksack. 'Now, keep the fire going, bolt the door after me, pull the quilt over you and don't let anybody in!' And out he went into the howling wind of the cold Christmas night.

The three boys did as they were told and rolled themselves under the quilt and listened to the quiet sizzling of the fire. After a while, they heard a knocking at the door. 'Let me in! Let me in!' came a high squeaky voice. Fritzel ran to the door and was about to draw the bolt.

'Remember what Father said!' cried Franzel. Hansel just peered out from a fold in the quilt, too frightened to move. Fritzel looked through a crack in the door and saw, standing in the snow, a very small man who was no bigger than little Hansel. His teeth were chattering and he was all a-shiver, from head to toe.

'Don't open it,' hissed Franzel. 'I must,' said Fritzel. 'He's freezing.' He drew the bolt and there stood the strangest little man they had ever seen. Under his high-peaked hat they saw a large red face with a broad nose, and under that a long red beard.

'You've kept me waiting a long time! Hogging all the fire and food to yourselves, I see!' said the stranger in his funny high voice, which didn't seem to belong to his short, stumpy body. He looked meaningfully at the poor fire, which was nearly out, and the empty table and the shelves where no food was stored.

'Well, the least you can do for me is to warm me up!' announced the little man. And with that, he climbed into the big straw bed. Franzel and Hansel drew back in amazement. Fritzel tried to explain that it wasn't for lack of welcome that they couldn't be more hospitable to the stranger, only that they had no firewood and no food left.

36

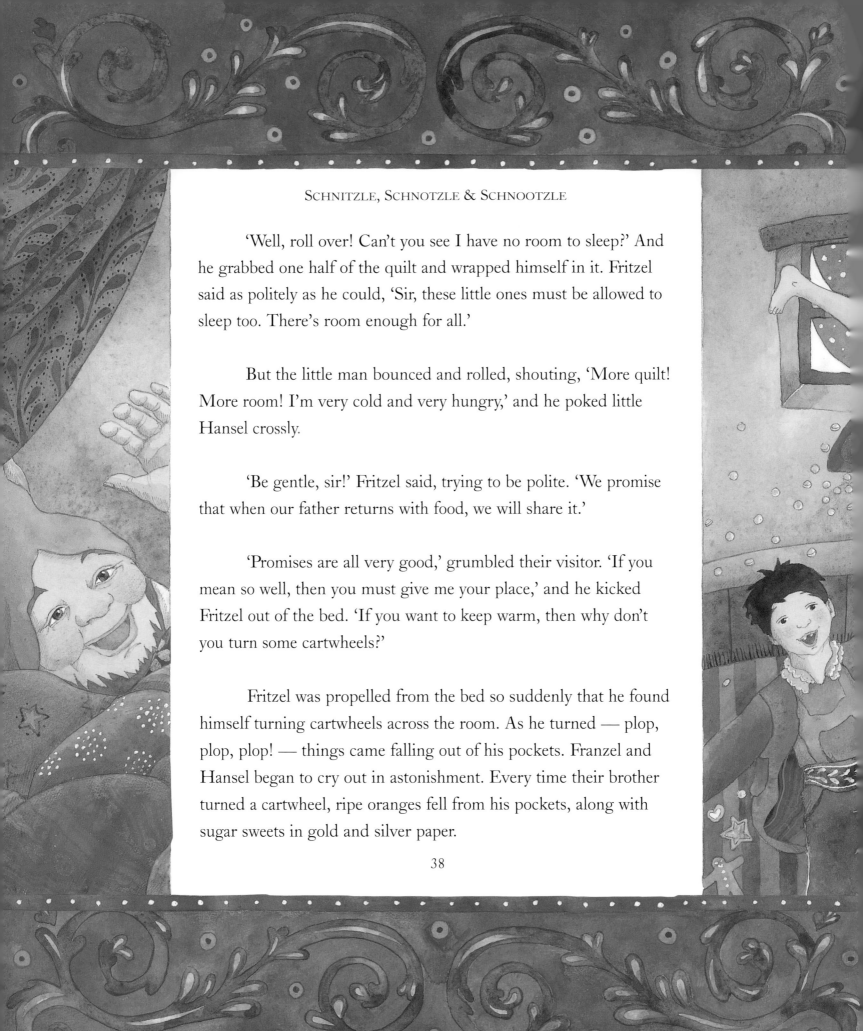

'Well, roll over! Can't you see I have no room to sleep?' And he grabbed one half of the quilt and wrapped himself in it. Fritzel said as politely as he could, 'Sir, these little ones must be allowed to sleep too. There's room enough for all.'

But the little man bounced and rolled, shouting, 'More quilt! More room! I'm very cold and very hungry,' and he poked little Hansel crossly.

'Be gentle, sir!' Fritzel said, trying to be polite. 'We promise that when our father returns with food, we will share it.'

'Promises are all very good,' grumbled their visitor. 'If you mean so well, then you must give me your place,' and he kicked Fritzel out of the bed. 'If you want to keep warm, then why don't you turn some cartwheels?'

Fritzel was propelled from the bed so suddenly that he found himself turning cartwheels across the room. As he turned — plop, plop, plop! — things came falling out of his pockets. Franzel and Hansel began to cry out in astonishment. Every time their brother turned a cartwheel, ripe oranges fell from his pockets, along with sugar sweets in gold and silver paper.

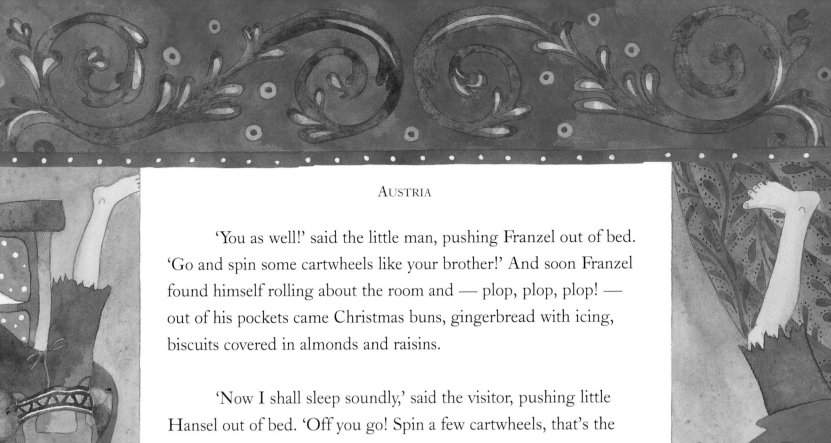

'You as well!' said the little man, pushing Franzel out of bed. 'Go and spin some cartwheels like your brother!' And soon Franzel found himself rolling about the room and — plop, plop, plop! — out of his pockets came Christmas buns, gingerbread with icing, biscuits covered in almonds and raisins.

'Now I shall sleep soundly,' said the visitor, pushing little Hansel out of bed. 'Off you go! Spin a few cartwheels, that's the thing!' Hansel soon found himself turning cartwheels too — something he had never done before — all about the floor. And out of his pockets — clang, clang, clankerty-clang! — came great fat golden coins, pouring on to the floor like hail.

The boys could not believe their good fortune. After they had danced about the room, singing for joy, Fritzel turned to say, 'Now we can offer you better Christmas cheer . . .' but he saw that the bed was quite, quite empty. Their visitor had vanished.

The boys gathered up their treasure: they set the shining oranges into bowls, put the buns and biscuits on the best platter, and poured the gold into as many dishes as they possessed. Then in walked their father, with bread, milk, noodles and meat. The soldiers had paid him in money and he had bought all that his family needed.

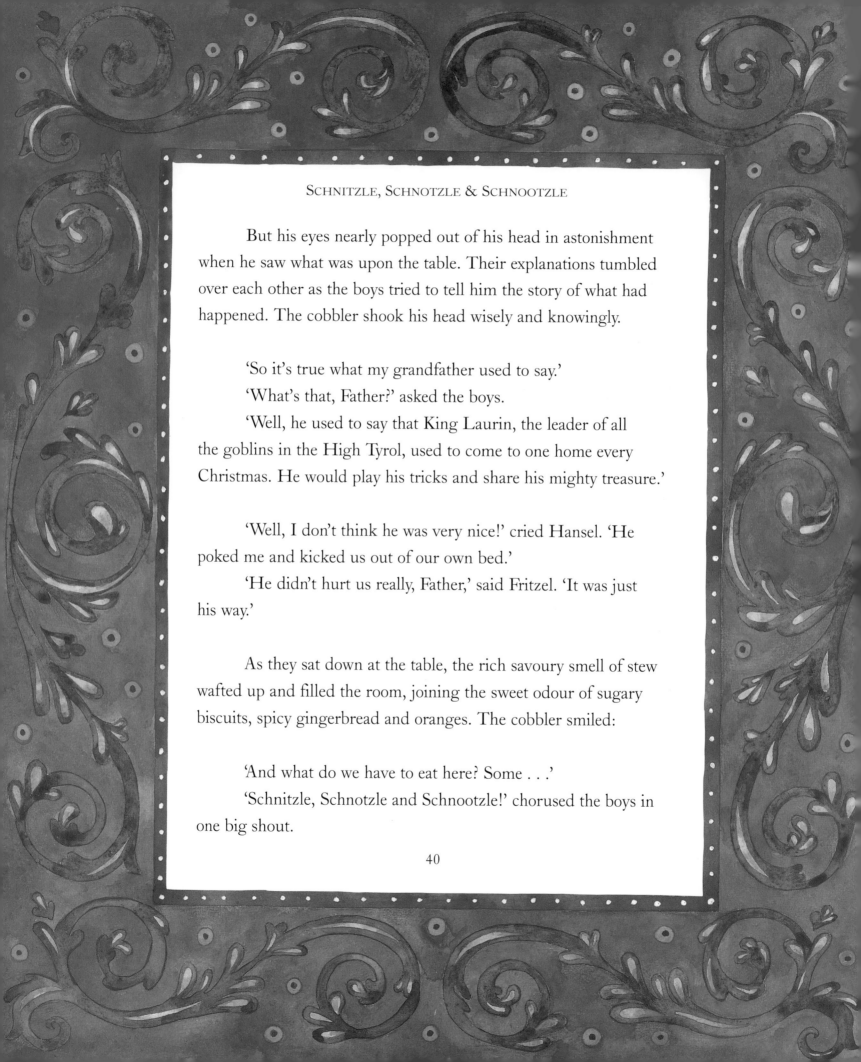

But his eyes nearly popped out of his head in astonishment when he saw what was upon the table. Their explanations tumbled over each other as the boys tried to tell him the story of what had happened. The cobbler shook his head wisely and knowingly.

'So it's true what my grandfather used to say.'
'What's that, Father?' asked the boys.
'Well, he used to say that King Laurin, the leader of all the goblins in the High Tyrol, used to come to one home every Christmas. He would play his tricks and share his mighty treasure.'

'Well, I don't think he was very nice!' cried Hansel. 'He poked me and kicked us out of our own bed.'
'He didn't hurt us really, Father,' said Fritzel. 'It was just his way.'

As they sat down at the table, the rich savoury smell of stew wafted up and filled the room, joining the sweet odour of sugary biscuits, spicy gingerbread and oranges. The cobbler smiled:

'And what do we have to eat here? Some . . .'
'Schnitzle, Schnotzle and Schnootzle!' chorused the boys in one big shout.

40

This New Year story is set in Russia in the nineteenth century, in a community of Orthodox Jews. In those days, as today among Orthodox Jews, the boys spent a lot of time learning scriptures and commentaries and it was rare for them to take a holiday. Prayer was a constant in everyone's lives, with special prayers to accompany every activity, morning to bedtime. A 'cantor' is the person who sings the prayers in a synagogue.

As well as the formal teachings of the scriptures, the children who grew up in the Jewish communities of Europe and Russia inherited a lot of folklore from the older generations. In this winter tale, Samuel's grandmother has a large repertory of stories that speak of an older wisdom. She tells her grandson something about the local trees that the rabbi has not taught him. Samuel's love of the trees leads him into great danger, but his song is one that we can all sing if we love whatever is endangered in our world.

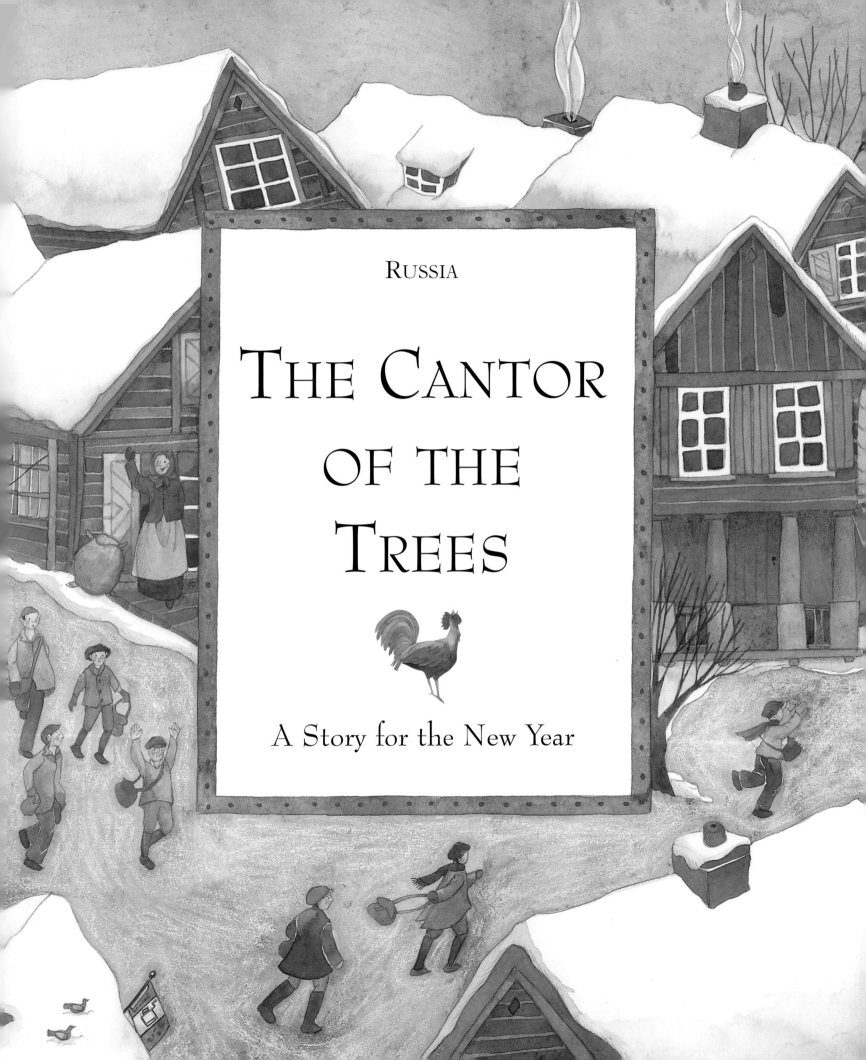

Russia

The Cantor of the Trees

A Story for the New Year

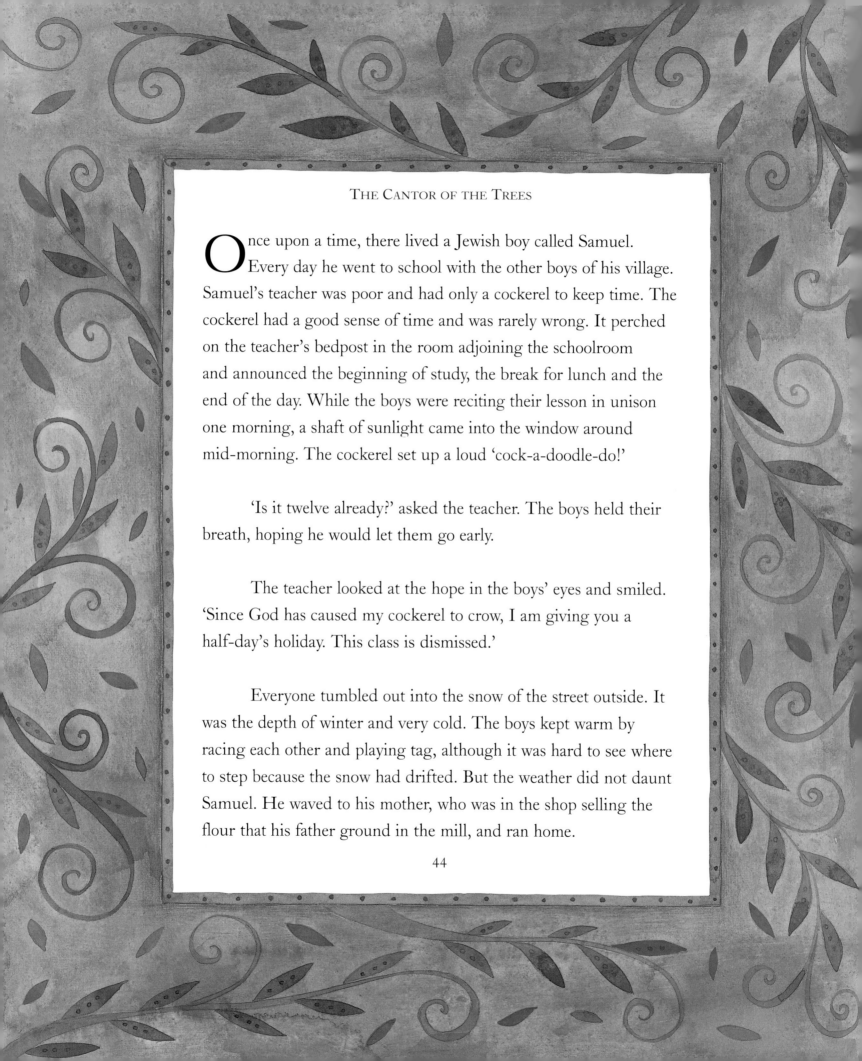

Once upon a time, there lived a Jewish boy called Samuel. Every day he went to school with the other boys of his village. Samuel's teacher was poor and had only a cockerel to keep time. The cockerel had a good sense of time and was rarely wrong. It perched on the teacher's bedpost in the room adjoining the schoolroom and announced the beginning of study, the break for lunch and the end of the day. While the boys were reciting their lesson in unison one morning, a shaft of sunlight came into the window around mid-morning. The cockerel set up a loud 'cock-a-doodle-do!'

'Is it twelve already?' asked the teacher. The boys held their breath, hoping he would let them go early.

The teacher looked at the hope in the boys' eyes and smiled. 'Since God has caused my cockerel to crow, I am giving you a half-day's holiday. This class is dismissed.'

Everyone tumbled out into the snow of the street outside. It was the depth of winter and very cold. The boys kept warm by racing each other and playing tag, although it was hard to see where to step because the snow had drifted. But the weather did not daunt Samuel. He waved to his mother, who was in the shop selling the flour that his father ground in the mill, and ran home.

The only person at home was his grandmother. Wrapped up in shawls and plump as a big loaf of bread, she scurried round and brought him a plate of treats. While he was eating, Samuel asked her: 'Why do you think the teacher let us come home early today?'

Grandmother settled back in her fireside chair, her eyes wide with wonder: 'Samuel, do you not remember it is the fifteenth day of Shevat, and you know what happens on that day?' Samuel shook his head. Grandmother knew many stories that even the rabbi had never heard, for she was the oldest person in the village. Samuel drew his stool closer to the stove to listen.

'This is the day when God makes a decision about every tree: which tree shall flourish and which will wither, which shall be fruitful and which will be struck by lightning or hail, which shall fall to the woodman's axe and which will be put into the fire — the Maker of the Universe decides all these things today.'

Samuel had never thought of the trees in this way before and it made his heart sad to consider that they would be judged. He had seen the rabbi's court when it gathered to judge people who had done wrong: it was a very solemn thing, but there was always a wise advocate to speak up for the wrongdoer.

'I wonder what the trees are doing about it?' He peered through the frost-covered window to look at the trees that grew around the back of his house. They were so much a part of his home that he couldn't imagine what it would be to lose the old mulberry tree on whose branches he would swing in the summertime. How he would miss the pretty birches that spread their skirts in the spring and the apple trees laden with golden fruit every autumn!

He thought to himself, 'Are they not sad in their hearts? I wonder if they are praying for mercy?'

Now, Samuel knew that when his own people needed help, if only ten of them could gather together and pray, God would hear their cries. Ten people made a minyan, a little circle of prayer. He tried to count the trees through the window to see if there were ten, but the wind was whipping the driving snow too hard to be able to tell.

Then he had an idea. He looked round. Grandmother was nodding off in her rocking chair. Quietly Samuel crept to the door and put on his coat and mittens and tied a scarf under his chin. He would just venture to the bottom of the garden to see how many trees there were, in case they needed his help.

The familiar little huddle of trees looked very different out here. The wind shook the trees so that the icicles hanging on their branches rang together. The long drops of ice made it look as if the trees were crying. The wind's howl sounded like the shofar, the ram-horn trumpet that was blown every Jewish New Year.

Samuel began to shake with dread. 'God is blowing the shofar before he gives judgement on the trees,' he whispered to himself. Quickly he strode forward into the deep drifts of snow and began to count the trees: the mulberry, five birches and three apple trees. They were all his friends, for the mulberry gave him purple berries in the summer and the apple trees gave him their crisp fruit in the autumn and the birch trees gave him their clean sap in the spring from which his mother would make lemonade. But there were only nine trees.

The icicles chimed together on the trees as if they were crying, 'Help us, Samuel! We are only nine and with you we are ten. Pray with us so that God will hear us!'

'Dear trees, since you have no one to make a tenth in your prayer circle, let me be your cantor! I know the prayers that must be sung.' So Samuel began to sing for them:

48

'Holy One, everyone who lives declares that you are King.
You search the hearts of all and reveal what is hidden.
Remember your trees, I pray.'
The wind blew the song from his mouth, so Samuel reached up his
hands and sang louder:
'Maker of the Universe, this day is holy.
Holy One, do not judge these trees harshly!'

Samuel's pure voice and the chiming icicles made one song.
He sang on with tears freezing upon his cheeks, his throat growing
sorer and sorer. Suddenly, he was grabbed. His grandmother and
mother, all bundled up with shawls and scarves, were shouting and
pulling at him, 'Samuel! Stop your screaming and come inside.'

For several days Samuel lay in bed, tossing and turning with
a high fever. The doctor came and gave him a bitter medicine that
his grandmother sweetened with honey. Even while he was asleep,
Samuel continued to sing. His parents were sick with worry. But his
grandmother sat with him, trying to do all that she could to keep life
in him. Then one day he opened his eyes and felt much better.

'What were you doing out in the cold in the middle of a
blizzard, Samuel?'

'I was making a tenth in the prayer circle of the trees, Granny, so that God wouldn't judge them but let them live.'

Grandmother shook her head and smiled: 'That is in the hands of the Almighty. Now sleep awhile and we will have food for you when you wake.'

Winter began to turn to spring before Samuel was well enough to go to school again, though he studied a little in bed. He often looked out of his window. There were many harsh winter days and several violent storms, but the trees continued to stand together, though there was little sign that they were still alive.

Gradually Samuel's cough started to fade and he felt strong again. Through his bedroom window he watched as the trees put on their blossom and their branches began to slowly green, first with buds and then with leaves again. He rejoiced in his heart that his prayer and that of the trees had been heard.

On the day that Samuel returned to school, the cockerel crowed aloud, and everyone heard the words distinctly: 'Behold the Cantor of the Trees!' For ever after, not just Samuel's schoolmates but all the villagers called him this — 'the Cantor of the Trees'.

51

In the old days, each of the Twelve Days of Christmas, from 26 December to 6 January, was considered to be an indicator of how each of the months of the coming year would turn out. People would look at the weather on the twelve days and make divinations, as well as playing games, sharing stories and making merry to help the health of the coming year.

This story from the Czech Republic reminds us that each month of the year has a special quality and that the twelve months together form the circle of the year, with its changing seasons reflecting the cycle of human existence, from the start of life (the winter solstice), through childhood (spring), adulthood (summer) to maturity (autumn), old age and death (winter again). The fortunes of the two sisters in the story also remind us that living with an attitude of respectfulness towards the natural world brings its own rewards, while abusing it can have dire consequences.

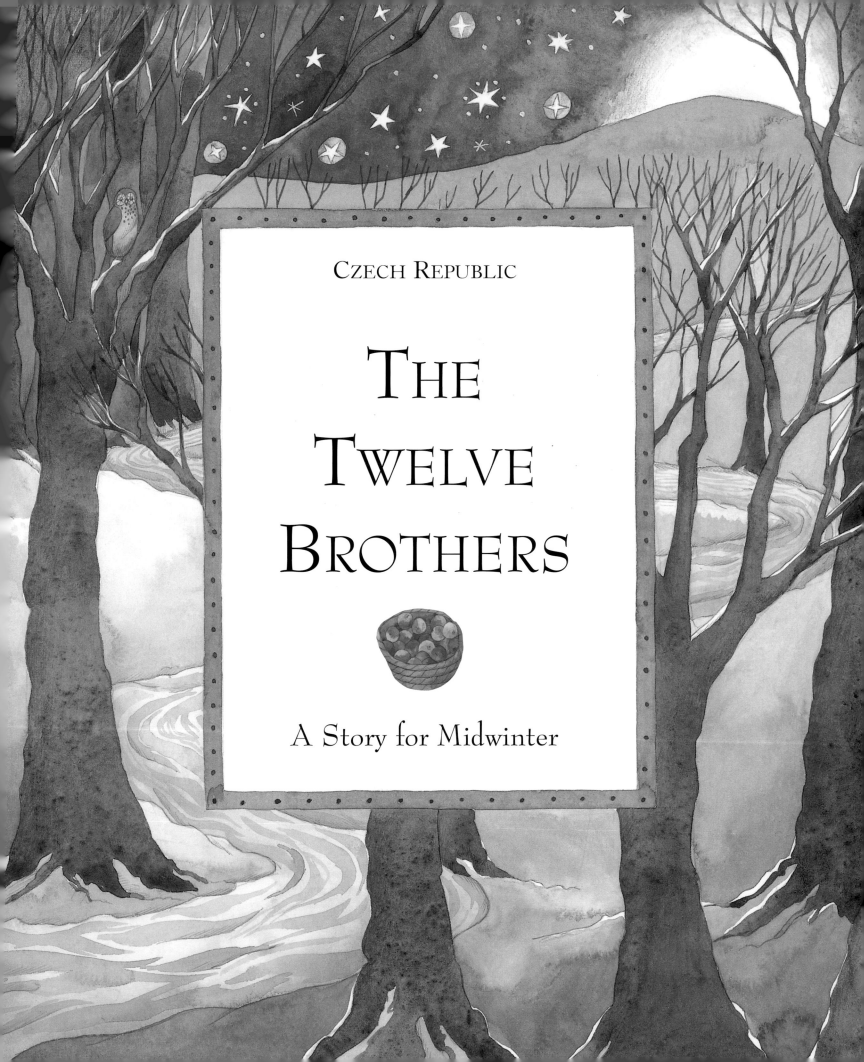

CZECH REPUBLIC

THE
TWELVE
BROTHERS

A Story for Midwinter

In a far-off forest, there once lived a widow with two little girls. One was her own daughter, Holena, while the other was her stepdaughter, Marusha. Holena was plain and spoiled. Pretty Marusha was made to do all the work. It was Marusha who went to the well at dawn to fetch water, Marusha who scrubbed and cooked, Marusha who spun and wove until darkness fell.

As the girls grew older, Marusha's reputation for beauty and hard work grew, as did Holena's reputation for idleness. Soon the widow realised that unless Marusha left, no one would ever want to marry lazy Holena. One bitter winter day, she called Marusha and said, 'Your sister needs some violets. Go out and fetch some,' fully intending that her stepdaughter should be devoured by the hungry wolves who roamed the forest.

'But where will I find violets in deepest winter?' cried Marusha, as she was thrust outside clad only in her thin dress. Shivering against the cruel north wind, she walked on till nightfall, fearful of the wolves' howling which seemed to be nearer with every step. She was about to give up and lie down in the snow and fall asleep for ever when she spied a beckoning light flickering on the hilltop ahead. She stumbled towards the welcoming flame, hoping that she would find shelter.

But when Marusha crested the hill, she drew back amazed. The scene before her was unlike anything she had ever seen before. It was like a story or song from the olden times. There before her was a great fire burning and, seated in silence around it on a circle of twelve great stones, were twelve men who all stared at her. They were quite unlike any men she had ever seen. Three were ancient men with long white beards, dressed in dark blue. The three cloaked in purple were middle-aged, and dressed in scarlet were three men in the prime of their lives. The last three were the youngest — vigorous youths dressed in clothes of white and green. Seated on the largest stone was one of the ancient men, with a club in his hand.

Marusha curtsied to him politely: 'Please, sir, might I be allowed to warm myself by your fire?' The ancient man had a deep, bell-like voice: 'Who are you, child, and why do you wander so late when the wolves are running?' Marusha told him about her errand for violets. 'You've come to the right place,' he told her, 'for we are the Twelve Brothers of the year. I am January, chief of them all. I cannot give you violets, but my younger brother March can.'

Old January rose, giving his place to one of the young men in green and white. As soon as young March sat in the High Seat, the snow immediately melted all around them, while the trees

began to bud and violets sprang up. 'Quickly, take them with you!' commanded young March, with a voice as piercing as the wind. Marusha picked the violets and, thanking him, rushed back home.

The widow couldn't believe her eyes when she saw the sweet purple flowers in Marusha's hands. 'Where did you find violets in January?' she demanded.

'Just on the hillside yonder,' was all Marusha would say.

A few days later the widow tried again. This time, she said to Marusha, 'Your stepsister needs some strawberries. Don't return without them!' Then she thrust Marusha out into the snow, without any shoes, thinking that, though it might have been possible to find a few early violets amid all this snow, her stepdaughter would certainly never find any strawberries.

Marusha returned to the silent figures on the hilltop where they sat around the fire. The Twelve Brothers listened seriously to her request, and again ancient January beckoned a younger brother to take his place. As soon as June in his scarlet clothes sat in the High Seat, glorious summer spread over the hill. Bees began to buzz around the white flowers of strawberry plants which quickly bloomed and became ripe red fruit in an instant. 'Take as many as you need,'

said June with a merry laugh. Marusha plucked the fruit, thanked June for his kindness and returned home, where her sister greedily ate them.

'And where did you find these, may I ask?' The widow's eyes glittered with suspicion.

'Under the trees in the shelter of the mountain,' was all Marusha would tell her.

A few days later, Holena begged her mother for apples, and the widow sent Marusha out into the snow again, without even a kerchief for her head. The wind blew stronger and the snow was crisp with ice as Marusha tramped along, trying not to notice the gleam of the wolves' eyes in between the dark trees. She came to the hilltop for a third time and again asked the Twelve Brothers for their help. January beckoned to one of the brothers and as soon as magnificent September in his purple cloak took the High Seat, suddenly autumn reigned. The leaves began to turn to orange, yellow and red, and an apple tree burst into fruit. 'Shake it, little daughter,' encouraged September, his smile as sweet and his voice as golden-ripe as fresh-pressed cider. Marusha shook the tree and down fell two perfect apples. Thanking September for his kindness, she took the fruit home.

Holena quickly gobbled up the apples, complaining that she wanted more, for they had been even more delicious than the strawberries. While the widow was dreaming up new ways to get rid of Marusha, Holena went to her mother and said, 'Mother, lend me your best fur coat and mittens. I want to go out. I'm sure that Marusha is keeping most of the fruit she finds for herself. I want to see where her secret supply is.'

With much fussing and complaining, the widow gave Holena permission to go into the cold, still night and look for herself. Holena wrapped herself up with the hooded fur coat and strode out. Eventually, her nose red with cold, she came puffing up the hill to the ring of stones on the top. Without greeting the Twelve Brothers or asking their permission, she pushed in among them and flopped down by the fire to warm herself.

Ancient January asked, 'Who are you, child, and what do you want here?' Holena irritably tossed her head, saying, 'It's none of your business, old fool!' January rose up in anger, his long beard bristling with frost. He uttered a long, wordless cry in a voice that seemed to be of one note with the winter winds that blew, and Holena fell back, very frightened. Then he swung his club over her head and immediately thick, fat flakes of snow began to fall.

59

Holena fled from the circle of stones, searching for the way she had come. But the thick white flakes had covered her footprints so that she couldn't find her way. As she ran terrified from the old man's rage, the snowflakes danced and spun about her in a shower of frost-flakes and the drifts grew deeper until she fell into the deepest hollow and was quite buried.

At home, the widow grew anxious for her daughter. Putting on her second-best fur coat and mittens, she went out to search for Holena. But January's rage had not yet abated. The snowstorm lasted all night, and nothing was seen of the widow or her daughter ever again.

Marusha did her work, cooked the dinner, fed the cow and filled her spindle with thread. When her stepmother and stepsister failed to return home that night, she looked out to see that the snow had ceased and that the stars hung crystal clear in the silence of the night. Strangely, she did not feel frightened or lonely, because she knew that the Twelve Brothers held the year in their hands. She lived with their blessing always in her heart, and when she married and became a mother, she taught her own children to see each month as an uncle who has different gifts to offer and always to be thankful for the special blessing of every season.

This story marks Twelfth Night, or the Epiphany, on 6 January. This is the night when, in the Christian tradition, the three wise men, or three kings, from the East — Caspar, Melchior and Balthasar — find the infant Jesus in the stable at Bethlehem. They present him with their gifts of gold, frankincense and myrrh, having followed the star that signified the birth of a great teacher.

'Babushka' is the Russian word for grandmother. The Babushka of this story is childless, but she loves children and keeps her house ready for any guest. She is also clever with her hands and makes fine little toys. When the three kings turn up on her doorstep, she is happy to welcome them. The three fine kings tell Babushka that they are looking for a baby who will become a great king. When she hears this, she is strangely moved, and wishes that she could take him a present. First, though, she has to tidy her house, so she sets off later than she had intended . . .

RUSSIA

BABUSHKA

A Story for Twelfth Night

Many years ago, in old Russia, there lived a woman called Babushka. Her house was the most beautifully kept in the whole village. From the brightly coloured gables on her roof, right down to her neat little garden, her house was a sight to behold.

Although she lived alone, Babushka was forever washing, cleaning, baking, cooking, painting and gardening, as if she were expecting a special guest. Although past the age of motherhood, she loved children and spent the long, cold winter months making fine little toys. Her hands were clever and strong, and her heart was pure and generous. Everyone in the village was very fond of her.

One evening, in the great expanse of the heavens, there appeared an enormous star with a trailing tail that moved across the sky. Everyone in the village was very excited about the new star, wondering what it could mean, but Babushka merely smiled and shook her head. 'Whatever it means, there is still the floor to be washed and the bread to be baked.'

But the next day, the meaning became plain. Over the hills beyond the village came a procession of strangers. They had come from far away. In the procession were three mighty kings. There was bearded Caspar in his crown of gold, riding upon a high-stepping

black horse. There was Melchior in his robes of white, fastened by a
jewel shaped like a star, riding upon a fine camel. And there was
Balthasar in his gold and red tunic, seated upon a magnificent white
stallion. Each of the kings carried a special treasure.

The kings' servants rode down into the village to find
lodgings. They asked the headman which house was most fitting for
their royal masters to sleep throughout that day, for the kings could
travel only by night. The headman longed to invite these grand
visitors to his own house, but he knew that it was too small and not
fine enough. He had fourteen children and the house was noisy and
not always as clean as it might be. So he said to the servants, 'Tell
your royal masters to ask at the house with the coloured gables.'

The kings dismounted outside Babushka's house and
knocked loudly. 'Good woman,' they said as she opened the door,
'we need to rest here this day until the star once more appears in the
sky. Do we have your permission to enter?'

Babushka pressed her hands to her cheeks in astonishment:
'Sirs, please come in. You are most welcome!' Soon the three kings
were sitting at her table and enjoying a meal of freshly cooked bread,
beetroot soup, pickled herrings and vegetables, washed down with

65

birch-sap beer. When they had eaten, Babushka invited them to sit around her fire and tell her about their journey.

'We are following the star whose glory has been foretold by my people for many years,' said Melchior, the firelight playing upon the starry jewel at his breast.

'Where does it lead?' asked Babushka.

Caspar spoke from the depths of his beard. 'We believe that the star will lead us to a king who is about to be born.'

Balthasar's dark eyes flashed. 'A king who is King of all the Universe. And we have brought him gifts.'

Babushka's eyes fell upon the precious things that the kings had brought with them, and her heart was strangely moved. If these great kings from countries far away thought it important enough to leave their kingdoms to find a humble newborn baby, then that child must be King indeed. If he were greater than they, then he was her King too.

'I wish I could bring him a present,' she said, almost to herself.

'Then why don't you come with us?' suggested Balthasar. Babushka looked up, startled, not realising that she had uttered her wish aloud.

While they slept, Babushka cleaned and tidied up the house. So many guests had left her with more work than usual. Could she really leave home and travel with the kings? What should she take as a gift? What things would she need for the journey?

At twilight, she wakened the sleeping kings, who got ready to leave. Balthasar stretched out his hand to include her in their procession. 'Are you coming, Babushka?'

'I have to find a gift. There is so much to get ready. I must tidy the house before I go. I will catch up with you.'

The kings went on their way, following the star. When she looked up and saw the star with her own eyes, Babushka knew that she really had to go. She rushed back into the house and began to look through her store of gifts. There were wooden animals, carved and painted; there were birch-bark boxes filled with ribbons, polished stones and sweets; there were nesting dolls that sat inside each other; there were whistles made of reeds. Which would be good enough for a newborn king?

Babushka simply could not decide which was best, so she packed them all in a big basket. She could decide as she travelled, or create something lovely along the way. By the time she had found

her wood-carving knife and paints, scissors and threads, and packed them away with her own few things for the journey, the cockerel was crowing. She gave a big yawn. How tired she was! She had been awake all day and night and now she fell into a deep slumber.

Babushka woke up at twilight and rushed out with her basket, keeping the glorious star ever before her. In every village, she asked after the three kings and which way they had gone. Babushka trudged onwards for days and months until she came to the royal palace of Jerusalem.

'At last! This must be where the newborn king will be found,' Babushka thought. She asked a guard outside the walls but he said, 'Yes, the three kings came here but they soon departed, hurrying onwards to a poor little place called Bethlehem.'

Off she went at once. She arrived at sunset and saw how the great star seemed to be directly overhead. Her heart leaped. This must be the place! At the inn she asked the innkeeper, 'Have the three kings been here?'

'Yes. They came to see the baby that was born in the stable here. But the kings have gone home now.'

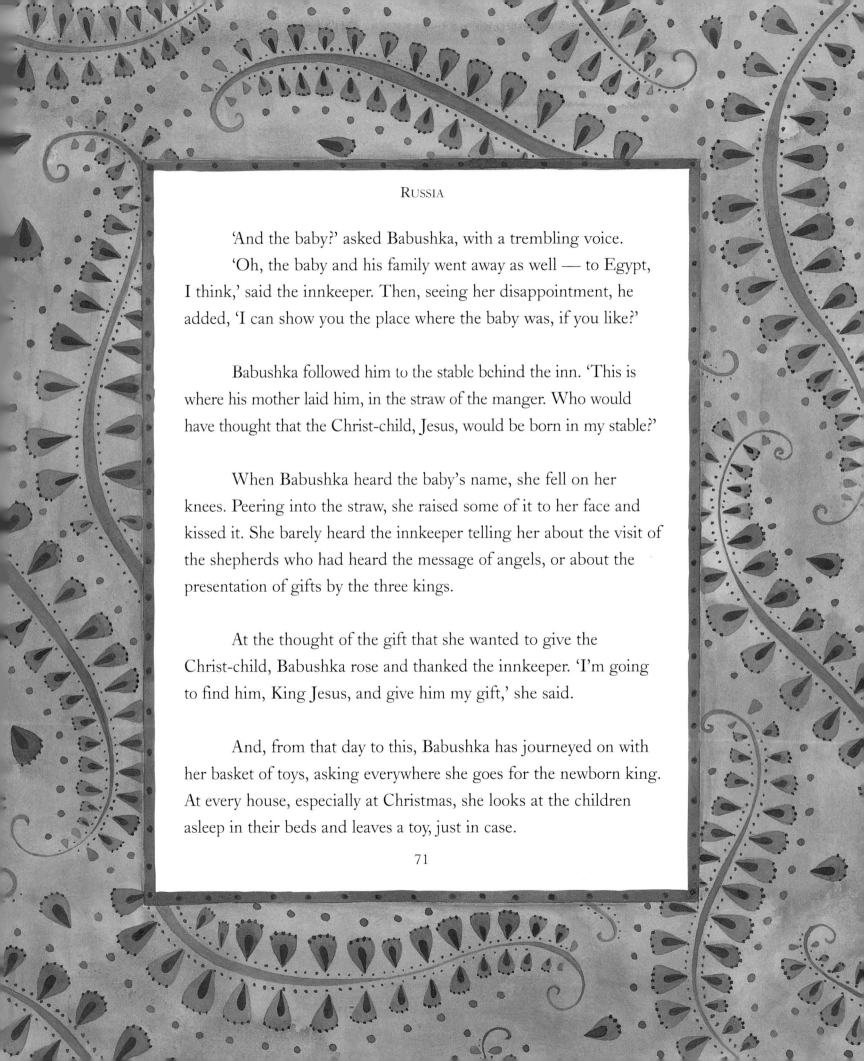

'And the baby?' asked Babushka, with a trembling voice.

'Oh, the baby and his family went away as well — to Egypt, I think,' said the innkeeper. Then, seeing her disappointment, he added, 'I can show you the place where the baby was, if you like?'

Babushka followed him to the stable behind the inn. 'This is where his mother laid him, in the straw of the manger. Who would have thought that the Christ-child, Jesus, would be born in my stable?'

When Babushka heard the baby's name, she fell on her knees. Peering into the straw, she raised some of it to her face and kissed it. She barely heard the innkeeper telling her about the visit of the shepherds who had heard the message of angels, or about the presentation of gifts by the three kings.

At the thought of the gift that she wanted to give the Christ-child, Babushka rose and thanked the innkeeper. 'I'm going to find him, King Jesus, and give him my gift,' she said.

And, from that day to this, Babushka has journeyed on with her basket of toys, asking everywhere she goes for the newborn king. At every house, especially at Christmas, she looks at the children asleep in their beds and leaves a toy, just in case.

As winter draws to a close, life starts to show above the ground in the new flowers of spring. For the Celts, Candlemas, on 2 February, was the day when the first spark of light entered the seeds that had been lying deep in the ground through the winter months. In many parts of the world, everything that lives and grows has a soul and a life force of its own, and deserves to be treated with respect. Even today, seeds are blessed before they are planted, and animals also receive blessings.

Of course, the light on which everyone on earth most depends is the sun. For the people of the far north, who spend winter in constant darkness, the return of the sun is a constant preoccupation. Many hold special ceremonies for the end of winter darkness as it signifies the return of spring, and the rebirth of nature. In this story from the Slavey people of Canada, the sun is kept in a bag by bears, who hibernate throughout the deepest winter months, and who will not bring warmth back to the world.

CANADA

THE
BAG OF
WARMTH

A Story for the Return of the Sun

Once, long ago, before there were any people, there was a very long winter. The sun was hidden behind black clouds and the snow just fell and fell. After three years of this, the animals got together to discuss what they should do.

As they gathered in council, they agreed that it was because of the lack of warmth that they were all so cold and hungry, but no one had any ideas about what they could do to change things for the better. Then the sharp-eyed wolf noticed that there were no bears at the council:

'Perhaps the bears know something that we don't? I wonder whether they're keeping all the warmth to themselves?'

So it was decided that seven animals should go and find the bears: the sharp wolf, the quick fox, the swift bobcat, the nosy wolverine, the wise pike, the secretive mouse and the strong dogfish should go and seek out the bears.

All of the animals knew that the bears lived somewhere in the upperworld, but how were they to find them? The wise pike suggested that all the questing animals sit around the fire and chant for help. As the different animals howled, barked, growled,

snuffled, squeaked and bubbled in their own voices, their song rose up like a wind, shaping the smoke from the fire into a pathway that enabled them to rise upwards and pass through a hole in the sky.

In the upperworld, they came to a big lake and a hut built beside it. The animals went in and found two young bear cubs huddling together by a fire.

'Where's your mother?' they asked the bear cubs.

'Mother's gone hunting,' they replied.

The animals looked around the hut and noticed lots of bags hanging from poles. The swift bobcat asked about the bag nearest him: 'What's in this bag?'

'Oh, Mother keeps the rain in that one,' said the bear cubs.

'What's in this one?' asked the secretive mouse.

'Oh, that one is full of winds.'

'And what's in this one?' asked the quick fox.

'That one has got fog in it,' replied the little bears.

Nosy wolverine sniffed loudly at the bag nearest to him: 'What about this one here?'

'Oh, we can't tell you that. Mother keeps that one secret and we're not allowed to tell.'

'You can tell us,' said the mouse, sweetly encouraging. 'We're your friends.'

The little bears put their paws over their noses, remembering how hard their mother could cuff them: 'Mother would be angry with us for telling you.'

Swift bobcat put his head on one side and said, 'But how would she know? We wouldn't tell her.'

The bear cubs were confused by this, but the animals were all very friendly so it seemed safe enough. 'In that bag she keeps the warmth,' they said shyly.

'Well, thank you kindly,' said the sharp wolf, grinning.

THE BAG OF WARMTH

The visitors all went outside to have a council meeting and decide what to do.

'We need a diversion so that the bag can be stolen,' said the wise pike.

'And we need to make sure that the bear won't run after us too fast once we've got the bag,' said the mouse, who had shorter legs than the rest of them.

The secretive mouse got up on the quick fox's back, and the fox ran to where the mother bear's canoe was moored on the other side of the lake. Mouse immediately set to gnawing through a good part of the paddle. Then the three of them watched and waited. Their patience was soon rewarded. The bear came running into view round the other side of the lake. Quick as a flash, swift bobcat changed himself into a plump caribou.

The bear smelled the caribou and began to yell for her children to come and help her catch some food. The cubs tumbled out of the hut and ran for her. Everything was happening just as the animals had hoped. The caribou-bobcat picked up his legs and began to lead the bears deep into the forest. As soon as the bears

78

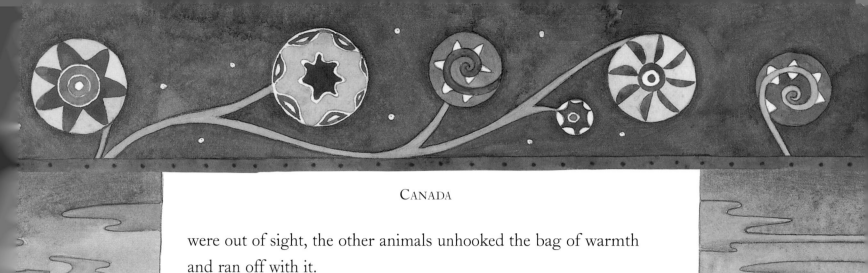

were out of sight, the other animals unhooked the bag of warmth and ran off with it.

Doubling back swiftly to the lake, the caribou-bobcat launched himself into the waters and swam across. The mother bear rushed after him. She told her cubs to wait for her on the bank, and then she jumped into her canoe and set off after the caribou-bobcat. But after she had taken just a few strokes, her paddle broke in two pieces. She fell head first into the river and down went the canoe.

The bobcat changed back into his own form when he reached the other side of the lake.

'Quickly now! Let's run before she can follow.'

The bag of warmth was very heavy and the animals had to take it in turns to drag it back to the hole where they had come into this world. They began to pull it more and more slowly, until they could almost feel the bear's breath on the back of their necks.

Finally the dogfish, who had done nothing yet, grabbed the bag with his mouth and pulled it through the hole with a shake

79

of his strong back. The bag and all the animals fell rapidly through the hole, tumbling down the path of smoke back into their own world below.

As soon as they had regained their breath, they tore open the bag. To everyone's relief, warmth rushed out and spread in all the directions. Ice and snow began to melt, the black clouds started to dissolve and the sun at last came out again. But the ice and snow was melting so fast that it caused a terrible flood. All the rivers flowed down to the seas so quickly that the seas rose all over the world.

The only thing left sticking out of the water was the tallest tree in the world. The animals climbed into its mighty branches and called for help. Deep in the depths of the sea, a giant fish heard their call and rose to the surface. It drank up the flood waters, until it had swollen to the size of a mountain. And there it remained as a great mountain for ever afterwards.

And so the sun dried up the land, the trees and flowers began to bloom again and summer was able to return to replace the winter cold. And that was how the animals brought the bag of warmth back to the earth.

Cailleach (pronounced 'KAL-yach') is a Gaelic word which means 'grandmother' or 'old woman'. There are all kinds of legends and stories about the Cailleach in England, Scotland, Ireland and Wales. Everyone is in agreement that she is the longest-living being in the land. Bride, or Bridie, is also an ancient goddess; over the years, her stories have been woven into those of the fifth-century Irish saint Brigit, of Kildare, a saint who is said to have visited parts of Britain.

These two great goddesses are brought together in this story because they are associated with the winter and spring months, and many of the legends about them concern the softening of winter's rigour and the coming of the spring. This story draws on Scottish folklore about both of these goddesses. It reminds us all of our intimate connection with the earth, as well as our constant dependency on the return of the spring and the warm months of the year.

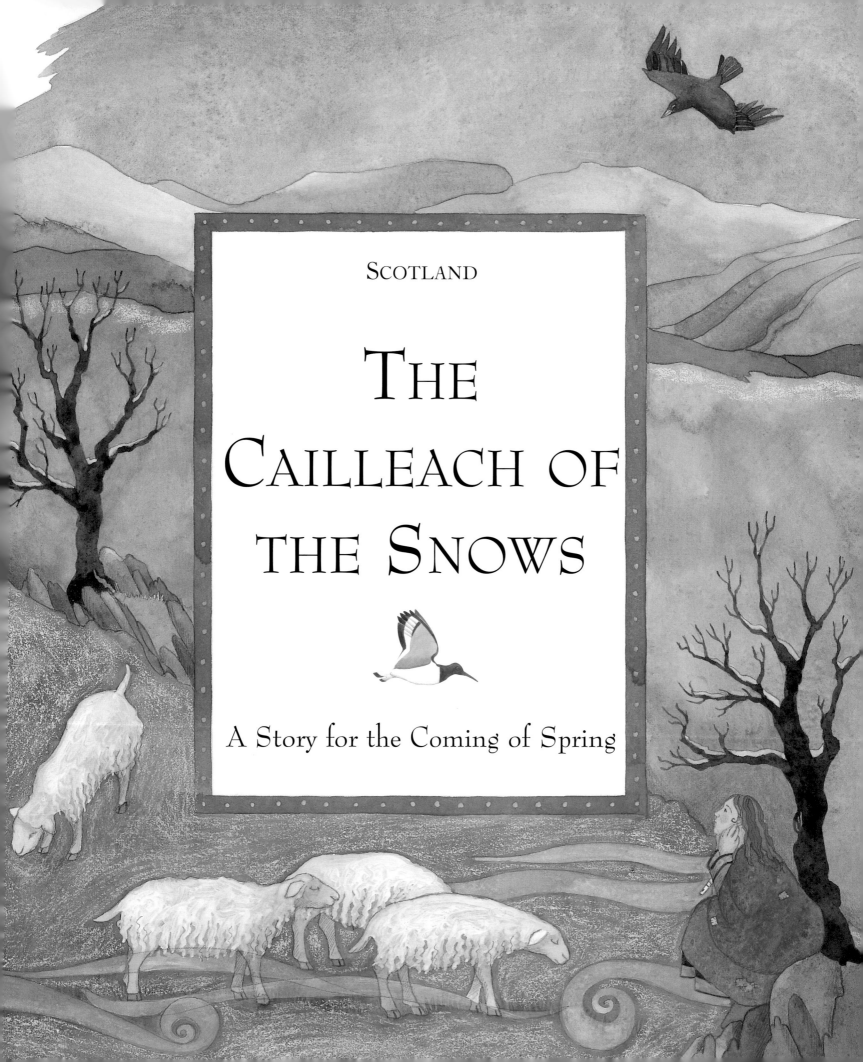

SCOTLAND

THE
CAILLEACH OF
THE SNOWS

A Story for the Coming of Spring

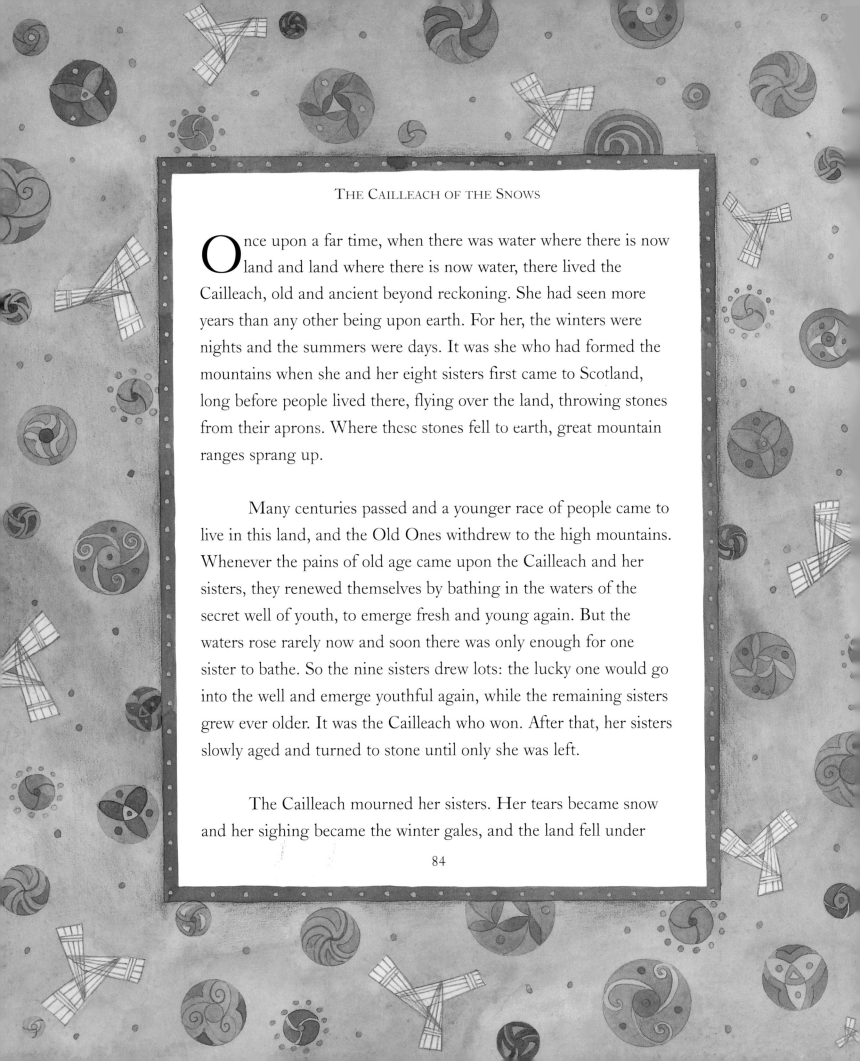

Once upon a far time, when there was water where there is now land and land where there is now water, there lived the Cailleach, old and ancient beyond reckoning. She had seen more years than any other being upon earth. For her, the winters were nights and the summers were days. It was she who had formed the mountains when she and her eight sisters first came to Scotland, long before people lived there, flying over the land, throwing stones from their aprons. Where these stones fell to earth, great mountain ranges sprang up.

Many centuries passed and a younger race of people came to live in this land, and the Old Ones withdrew to the high mountains. Whenever the pains of old age came upon the Cailleach and her sisters, they renewed themselves by bathing in the waters of the secret well of youth, to emerge fresh and young again. But the waters rose rarely now and soon there was only enough for one sister to bathe. So the nine sisters drew lots: the lucky one would go into the well and emerge youthful again, while the remaining sisters grew ever older. It was the Cailleach who won. After that, her sisters slowly aged and turned to stone until only she was left.

The Cailleach mourned her sisters. Her tears became snow and her sighing became the winter gales, and the land fell under

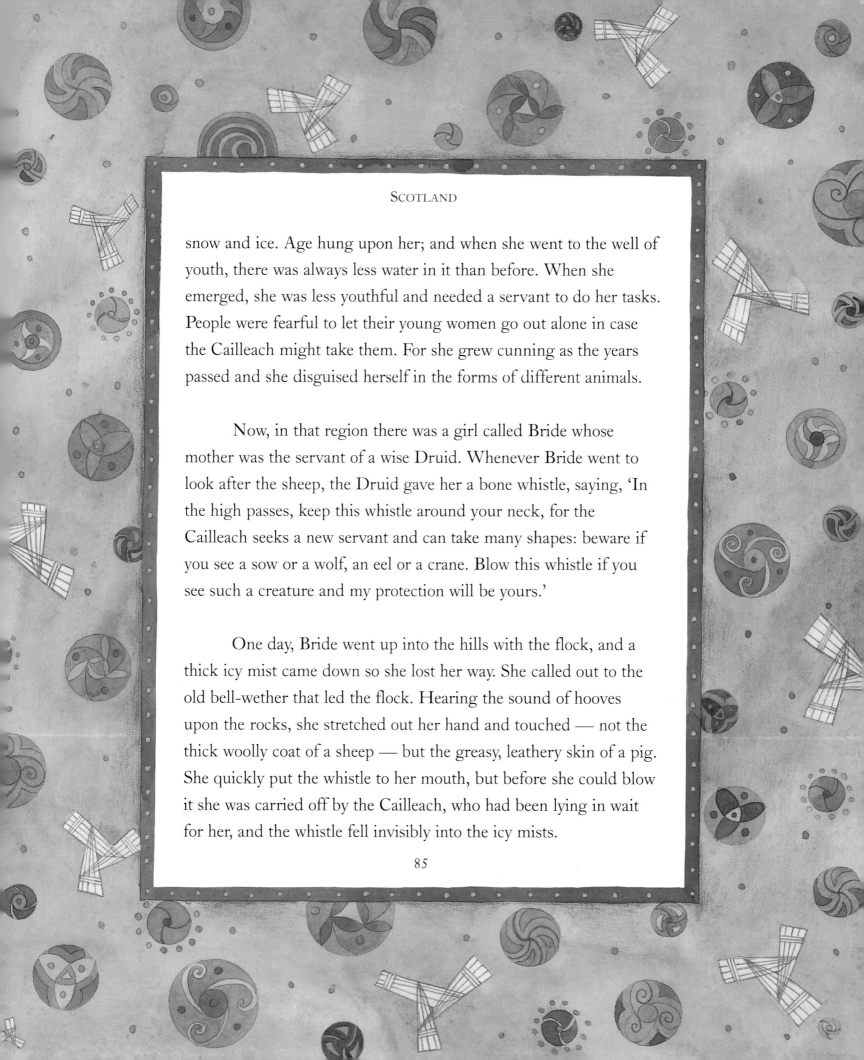

snow and ice. Age hung upon her; and when she went to the well of youth, there was always less water in it than before. When she emerged, she was less youthful and needed a servant to do her tasks. People were fearful to let their young women go out alone in case the Cailleach might take them. For she grew cunning as the years passed and she disguised herself in the forms of different animals.

Now, in that region there was a girl called Bride whose mother was the servant of a wise Druid. Whenever Bride went to look after the sheep, the Druid gave her a bone whistle, saying, 'In the high passes, keep this whistle around your neck, for the Cailleach seeks a new servant and can take many shapes: beware if you see a sow or a wolf, an eel or a crane. Blow this whistle if you see such a creature and my protection will be yours.'

One day, Bride went up into the hills with the flock, and a thick icy mist came down so she lost her way. She called out to the old bell-wether that led the flock. Hearing the sound of hooves upon the rocks, she stretched out her hand and touched — not the thick woolly coat of a sheep — but the greasy, leathery skin of a pig. She quickly put the whistle to her mouth, but before she could blow it she was carried off by the Cailleach, who had been lying in wait for her, and the whistle fell invisibly into the icy mists.

The Cailleach took Bride back to her draughty cave and set her to milking the herd of deer that were stockaded in the glen. Many hundreds and thousands of years had passed since reindeer roamed these glens; now there were only the red deer of the mountains. And Bride, who had been used to milking the sheep, now tended the deer and made cheese from their milk instead, and always she dreamed of home.

The months passed, and though Bride searched for the lost whistle, she never could find it. One day, the Cailleach assumed the form of a crane and took Bride down to the seashore to fish with a baited line. 'Fill this creel with fish before nightfall,' commanded the Cailleach. 'I will fish along the loch-side and fetch you back before dark.'

With shivering fingers, Bride baited the line with worms and wept, longing for her mother. As she cried upon the seashore, a black and white bird with a long red beak drew steadily nearer. 'Klee-ee, klee-ee!' it called. 'Klee-ee, klee-ee!' Bride realised it was trying to win her attention so she stopped crying and smiled at the bird. At this, the bird spoke, for it was none other than the Druid, who had come to her in the shape of an oystercatcher. 'Keep fishing, Bride, and listen to me! I have been searching for you for the better part of a year. The time of the Cailleach is passing, and the time of Bride is coming. Do as I say and not only will you be free from the Cailleach's service but you will also inherit her wisdom and power. She cannot survive many more winters without renewal.'

'What must I do?' whispered Bride, taking the fish off the line and placing them in the creel.

'Three things will bring you freedom. First of all you must discover her secret name; then you must look for the well of youth; lastly you must overcome her iron grip upon winter so that the spring may speedily return. To find out her secret name, you must ask her how long she has lived. Listen carefully to all that she tells you and report it to me, for I will come to you again.'

Later that evening, Bride made up the fire and gave the Cailleach a beaker of deer's milk, saying shyly, 'You must have lived a very long time, great Cailleach . . .'

'Ah! child, I have lived from before the time when the seas were once land and the land was once water. Before the mountains raised their peaks, and the glens filled with lochs, the Daughter of the Skies was born,' said the Cailleach.

'Is that your name?' asked Bride, but the Cailleach turned from her sadly and would say no more.

The oystercatcher came to Bride once again and listened to what the Cailleach had said.

'The Cailleach's secret name is Nic Neven, the Daughter of the Skies,' said the Druid. 'Armed with this knowledge, you will be able to find the place of her secret renewal and ensure that she cannot use it. The time is near when she must renew herself or perish. Watch and follow her closely. But now you must gather rushes from the loch and weave them into this shape.' The bird drew in the earth with its beak, making a three-spoked cross. 'You will need this sign to seal the well until the Cailleach goes to her long sleep. The weaker she becomes, the more easily you will overcome her.' The oystercatcher then taught her what to do and what to say.

When the Cailleach dozed in her cave, Bride's busy fingers wove the three-spoked cross from the rushes she had hidden. The very next day, long before dawn, the Cailleach went in the shape of a narrow grey wolf to inspect the well of youth, and Bride followed her at a distance.

But the time for the waters to rise had not yet come and the Cailleach-wolf slunk away down the mountain. Bride went to the well and, just as the Druid had taught her, she laid the cross woven out of rushes upon the opening of the well and said:

'In the name of the ancient one, Nic Neven,
I seal this well with the star of heaven.
By spark of sun and ray of fire,
May the waters of youth rise up no higher,
Until I call with voice of power;
Then waters rise and mountain flower!'

Then Bride said to the oystercatcher, 'I have done all that you told me, but how can her iron grip upon winter be loosened?'

The Druid said, 'Cut a birch wand from the tree that grows at the head of the glen and teach the Cailleach the Jig of the Mill Dust. It is many hundreds of years since she danced and she will be delighted. You must show her all the steps and, putting the birch wand in her hand, tell her that she must practise on you. Make sure you fall down first and let her strike your hands, feet and mouth with the wand. When she does that, then you will be dead for a short time. But never fear, for I will be nearby to whistle the music.

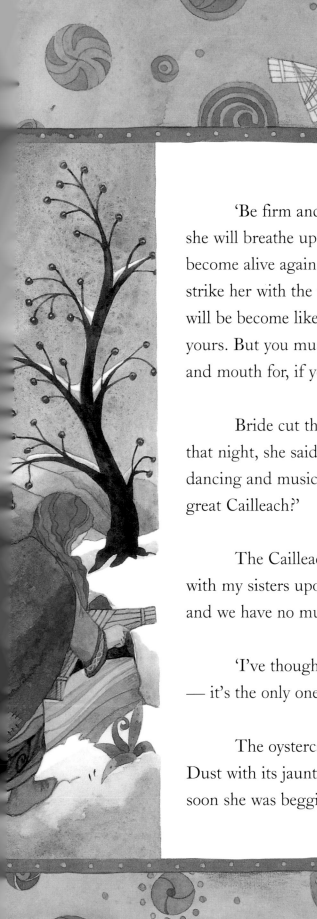

'Be firm and brave, for she will want to dance in turn, and she will breathe upon your hands, feet and mouth so that you become alive again. When it is her turn to fall down, you must strike her with the wand upon her hands, feet and mouth, then she will be become like stone and all her power and wisdom will be yours. But you must be sure never to breathe upon her hands, feet and mouth for, if you do, she will awaken again.'

Bride cut the birch wand and hid it under her cloak. Later that night, she said to the Cailleach, 'The nights are long without dancing and music. I wonder whether you would like to dance, great Cailleach?'

The Cailleach sighed, 'Hoo-a hoo! It is long since I danced with my sisters upon the first grass of the glens. I am too old now and we have no music.'

'I've thought of that. I've taught this bird the tune of a dance — it's the only one he can whistle.'

The oystercatcher obediently whistled the Jig of the Mill Dust with its jaunty rhythm. The Cailleach's foot began to tap and soon she was begging to be taught the dance.

Bride brought out the wand from the woodpile and showed the Cailleach how the dance went. 'First we come together, then we step away, then we weave and change places,' she said, banging the birch wand upon the ground to the rhythm of the steps. Soon the Cailleach was breathless. 'It's a very vigorous dance!' she puffed.

Bride smiled, 'Yes, but we take turns having a rest like this. First one of us taps the other on the head with the wand and the other falls down. Then the one who is still standing will touch the other on the hands, and they do a little dance of their own; then on the feet and lastly on the mouth. And then when the one on the floor is very still, the other one breathes on to their hands, feet and mouth and then they stand up again and change places. Have you got your breath back now? Well, why don't you try holding the wand and I will lie down first while you're learning the dance. Then, you can take your turn lying down and rest as long as you like.'

'Good!' said the Cailleach. And they began. First, she tapped Bride on the head and down she fell to the floor. With the wand, the Cailleach made Bride's hands and feet do a little dance on their own while she lay upon the ground, her heart pounding with fear. She trusted the Druid, but she didn't know that the Cailleach would remember to breathe upon her hands, feet and mouth again. For if she didn't, then Bride would be dead for ever. Then the Cailleach tapped her on the mouth with the wand, and Bride felt the breath dry up within her. The oystercatcher whistled on, but Bride heard no more until the Cailleach began to breathe upon her mouth, and the life came back into her and she leaped up gladly.

'Now it's your turn to dance!' said the Cailleach, and they began again. This time, Bride struck the Cailleach with the wand and she fell to the ground so that the earth itself shuddered. The wand made the Cailleach's hands and feet do a little dance of their own, which made the needles on the pine trees tremble and the icicles hanging from the rocks began to shiver. But these were the last movements that the Cailleach made, for when Bride touched her mouth with the birch wand, the Cailleach turned to cold, unmoving stone.

The oystercatcher bowed his head to Bride, saying, 'The power of the Cailleach is now yours. Use the wand wisely, for, as the light lengthens, so the cold strengthens.'

Bride felt that great power within herself and promised then and there to be the helper of all beings who were in trouble. She called out in a loud voice:

93

'Nic Neven's power is overthrown!
Rise up waters from deep down stone!
By ray of fire and spark of sun,
May winter's whiteness be undone!
Life be renewed by springtime's power;
Now black ice crack and mountain flower!'

Bride raised the wand and the wheel of rushes that covered the well of youth flew into the sky like a spinning sun. The waters of the well swept up on the power of her song and fell as rain upon the land, melting the ice and snow. Upon the mountainside, the first green shoots of snowdrops pierced the hard ground and everywhere people gave thanks and welcomed Bride back among them.

Every springtime, we still weave Bride's cross out of rushes, to celebrate the turning wheel of the seasons, and to remind us to call upon Bride when we need help. To this day, the oystercatcher is known as Gille Bhrighid, or Bride's Servant.

The winters are not so hard as they once were and the Cailleach rarely moves from her confinement of stone. But, if the snows are heavy, people still say that the Cailleach walks the land once more.

94

SOURCES

THE LONELY BOATMAN
This story is based upon an oral recitation of a ghost story heard twenty-two years ago at a storytelling festival. I remember as a child being both scared and excited whenever I read stories with a time-slip: this same frisson happens to me today. Of course, Samhain is an occasion when the boundaries of time melt, when ancestors and faeries can come among us or when we can visit their world, as poor Hamish does!

THE WINTER CABIN
Throughout the world there are many stories that tell of how a group of domesticated animals gets together to outwit wild animal predators. These stories reveal how the animals' instinctive powers are enhanced by human characteristics to somehow survive the winter.

From 'The Animal's Winter Home' in Alexander Afanasiev's collection *The Three Kingdoms: Russian Folk Tales*, Raduga Publishers, Moscow, 1981 (translated by Raduga Publishers).

SCHNITZLE, SCHNOTZLE & SCHNOOTZLE
As with many European folk tales, there is often a strong bond between shoemakers and elves, faeries and dwarfs, who seem well disposed to help those who work with leather. Is there a connection between the repairers of soles and the helpers of souls, I often wonder?

From Sawyer, Ruth, *The Long Christmas*, Viking Press, New York, 1941.

THE CANTOR OF THE TREES
When we are young, it often seems as if it is only adults who have the power to change things, but this inspiring story shows how a boy's heartfelt prayers are just as important as those of his congregation.

From Eisenberg, Azriel & Leah Ain Globe, *The Secret Weapon and other stories of Faith and Valor*, Soncino Press, London, 1966.

THE TWELVE BROTHERS
The character of each month distinctively reveals the changing seasons, bringing us new gifts and insights every year. In this story, a cruel stepmother's requests for out-of-season fruits bring its heroine into the circle of the Twelve Brothers who spin the seasons to ensure her safety.

From Williams, Harcourt, *Tales From Ebony*, Nattali & Maurice Ltd, London, 1947.

BABUSHKA
As well as the Three Wise Men who brought gifts to the stable at Bethlehem, we can add the figure of the Wise Woman. Both Russian Babushka and her Italian counterpart, Befana, are wise grandmothers whose chief concern is the happiness of children.

From Robbins, Ruth, *Baboushka and the Three Kings*, illustrated by Nicolas Sidjakov, Houghton Mifflin, 1960.

THE BAG OF WARMTH
Throughout North America there are many stories that relate how the raven stole back the sun and so brought about the end of winter. This story shows again how a group of animals pool their strengths and abilities to bring help to the world.

From 'Legends of the Slavey Indians of the MacKenzie River' in *The Journal of American Folklore*, Volume 14, 1901.

THE CAILLEACH OF THE SNOWS
This is a story of my own invention from the oral myths and traditions surrounding Bride and the Cailleach. For more background see:

Mackenzie, Donald A., *Wonder Tales From Scottish Myth and Legend*, Blackie & Son Ltd, London, 1917.

Matthews, Caitlín, *King Arthur and the Goddess of the Land*, Rochester IL., Inner Traditions, 2002.

Barefoot Books
step inside a story

At Barefoot Books, we celebrate art and story that opens the hearts
and minds of children from all walks of life, focusing on themes that
encourage independence of spirit, enthusiasm for learning and respect
for the world's diversity. The welfare of our children is dependent on
the welfare of the planet, so we source paper from sustainably managed
forests and constantly strive to reduce our environmental impact.
Playful, beautiful and created to last a lifetime, our products combine
the best of the present with the best of the past to educate our
children as the caretakers of tomorrow.

www.barefootbooks.com

Caitlín Matthews is the author of many books on sacred lore and Celtic traditions. She was born a week after Christmas and has always loved the snow and stories about midwinter. A writer, singer and storyteller, Caitlín lives in Oxford, England. She is also the author of *The Barefoot Book of Princesses*.

www.hallowquest.org.uk

Helen Cann loves to travel to cold places. She has seen the Northern Lights, slept in an igloo, eaten reindeer with Sami herders and helped crew a boat sailing from Iceland to Sweden via the Faroe Islands. She has painted in studios of all shapes and now stirs up inspiration above a milkshake shop in Brighton, England. Helen's award-winning illustrations have graced the pages of many Barefoot Books stories, including *Little Leap Forward*.

www.helencann.co.uk